"Why should I want what other men have bought?"

Caught in a spasm of confusion and self-loathing, Olivia sought refuge in the avaricious identity Edward had given her.

"Perhaps because you know you can never afford it," she said in a voice that seemed far too biting to be her own.

His hands tightened on her for a moment. He was in control again; she could see that in the coolness of both his smile and his eyes.

"Don't ever offer a challenge, Olivia," he said softly. "You might find I'll take you up on it!"

SANDRA MARTON has always believed in the magic of storytelling and the joy of living happily ever after with that special someone. She wrote her first romance story when she was nine and fell madly in love at sixteen with the man she would eventually marry. Today, after raising two sons and an assortment of furry, four-legged creatures, Sandra and her husband live in a house on a hilltop in a quiet corner of Connecticut.

Books by Sandra Marton

HARLEQUIN PRESENTS
1457—LOST IN A DREAM
1574—ROARKE'S KINGDOM
1637—THE CORSICAN GAMBIT
1660—ROMAN SPRING

Don't miss any of our special offers. Write to us at the following address for information on our newest releases.

Harlequin Reader Service
U.S.: 3010 Walden Ave., P.O. Box 1325, Buffalo, NY 14269
Canadian: P.O. Box 609, Fort Erie, Ont. L2A 5X3

SANDRA MARTON

A Woman Accused

Harlequin Books

TORONTO • NEW YORK • LONDON
AMSTERDAM • PARIS • SYDNEY • HAMBURG
STOCKHOLM • ATHENS • TOKYO • MILAN
MADRID • WARSAW • BUDAPEST • AUCKLAND

ISBN 0-373-11736-1

A WOMAN ACCUSED

Copyright © 1993 by Sandra Myles.

First North American Publication 1995.

This edition published by arrangement with Harlequin Enterprises B.V.

® and TM are trademarks of the publisher. Trademarks indicated with ® are registered in the United States Patent and Trademark Office, the Canadian Trade Marks Office and in other countries.

Printed in U.S.A.

CHAPTER ONE

OLIVIA was running late. There was nothing unusual about that, but with summer gone and autumn on the way it seemed that everyone who'd ever given a passing thought to redecorating a living-room or a flat had suddenly decided now was the time and had come racing into Interiors by Pierre, bearing swatches of fabric or chips of paint that just had to be matched, and would it be too much to have the job done yesterday?

It made for awfully good business, Pierre said in his high-pitched voice. But it had played havoc with Olivia's schedule. Now she was late for her lunch with Ria.

And it wasn't just any lunch, she thought ruefully as she hurried along Fifth Avenue. It was their annual birthday lunch, and Olivia had sworn on everything that was holy that she wouldn't be late.

Well, she had done her best. It was just that it hadn't been quite good enough. Not that Ria would be surprised.

'We both know you're going to be late, Livvie,' she'd said, tossing her thick mane of dark hair. 'That old goat works you like a slave, even though he knows you're the only reason he has so many customers. Honestly, Livvie, it's time you went into business for yourself.'

Olivia smiled a little as she remembered those words. She did work hard at Interiors by Pierre, but then that, along with the talent Monsieur Pierre was so loath to admit she possessed, was why she'd gone from shop girl to design assistant in three years. As for opening her own shop—you couldn't borrow enough money to do it right without assets to pledge as collateral.

'But if you had collateral you wouldn't need a loan,' Ria had said, and they'd both laughed.

It was ridiculous, but it was reality. Olivia hadn't really expected her friend to understand. Ria had been born into a world of privilege and wealth; her idea of hard work was her noon-to-six, three-day-a-week stretch at a trendy avant-garde art gallery—which was why it was always easy for her to be on time for lunch.

'You won't want to be late this time,' she'd said with a giggle, almost as if she were still ten instead of about to turn twenty-six. 'Just wait until you see your birthday present!'

Olivia's senses had gone on alert as she thought of the silk scarf she'd bought for Ria.

'Remember what we agreed?' she'd said warningly. 'No more expensive gifts. That watch you gave me last time was gorgeous, but——'

'You're so silly, Livvie. What's the point of having money if I can't spend it on the people I love?'

It had been a sticking point between them for years, Olivia trying to make Ria see that she couldn't possibly match her oldest friend's extravagance and Ria explaining that her gifts were meant to bring pleasure, and each encounter ended the same way.

'You don't like it?' Ria would say, her eyes clouded, and by the time Olivia had finished assuring her that it wasn't that at all it was always too late. 'Good,' Ria would declare happily. 'Then enjoy, darling!'

Olivia sighed as she hurried towards the restaurant. Ria had teased her about this year's gift.

'It's right up your alley,' she'd said. 'It's practical. Pragmatic. Why, it's downright sensible. You just get to Luigi's on time and see if you don't agree.'

Now, as Olivia glanced down at the expensive diamond and gold watch encircling her slender wrist—Ria's gift of last year and one she rarely wore—she made a face. She wasn't going to get there on time, that was certain. She was already a quarter of an hour late. Of course, she thought hopefully, the watch might not be keeping time properly. She hadn't worn it in months, it was far too expensive to wear every day, and besides it was just a little flashy for her tastes...

Who was she kidding? A watch like this would rather die than be inaccurate. She was definitely late, and who knew how much further it was to Luigi's?

'It's this darling little place just off Fifty at Fifth-sixth,' Ria had said, but Ria's ability to judge distances hadn't noticeably improved any in the fifteen years they'd known each other. 'Just off Fifth' could mean anything from around the corner to Sutton Place—although, Olivia thought, suppressing a grin, Ria wouldn't very likely pick a bit of real estate as far removed as that. Luigi's would be located somewhere along this golden stretch of New York pavement, tucked between the bustle of Fifth Avenue and the quiet grandeur of Park. Its décor would be handsome, the food luscious, the wine list intimidating—and perhaps this time, Olivia thought with a twinge of guilt, she and Ria would have more to say to each other than the last. They'd known each other forever. Surely they still had things in common, now that they'd put away their toys.

Ah! Olivia's pace quickened, her high heels tapping lightly against the pavement. There it was! A discreet black sign, just in the middle of the block, with the restaurant's name inscribed in gold script. She'd arrived, and only twenty minutes past the appointed hour.

A uniformed doorman appeared from out of nowhere; he held open the brass-studded door, bowing grandly as if she were royalty.

'Thank you,' she murmured, fighting back the urge to put a nervous hand to her glossy, dark brown hair. It was probably wind-tossed, the shoulder-length, almost untameable curls even wilder-looking than usual, she thought irritably, annoyed not at her hair nor the unctuously smiling doorman but at herself for still feeling such a sudden twinge of nerves at the thought of stepping inside a place that was so obviously a haven for those born to the good life.

What on earth had brought that on? It was a long
time since anyone had teased her about not belonging,
longer still since she'd given a damn. Her chin lifted.
Besides, in the emerald-green silk suit she'd designed and
made she'd look as good as any woman in this posh little
café.

And it was posh, she thought as she stepped inside.
The tiny entry foyer was done in black and white marble,
with the scheme repeated in the dining-room that opened
beyond, all of it heightened by accents of burgundy and
pink. The room was dim and intimate, with a mirrored
bar to the right and deep banquettes beyond. Music
played softly in the background, and the air bore just
the faintest hint of good wine and perfume.

She glanced at her watch again as she waited for the
head waiter. Perhaps Ria was already seated. Olivia
stepped forward a bit, just into the bar, and peered into
the main room. Was that a dark head at a table off to
the side? She stood on tiptoe, then took another step
forward...

The man stepped back from the bar at just that instant. Olivia had time only to register the grey wool
jacket, the flash of a highball glass in a masculine hand,
and then a sudden rush of cold liquid splashed across
her silk dress and down her skirt.

She cried out, almost in unison with a deep voice that
muttered something far more explicit, and when she
looked up she was staring first at a splattered dark silk
tie, then at a face as cold and aggressively masculine as
any she'd ever seen.

'Dammit, woman, why don't you look where you're
going?'

Olivia's mouth dropped open. 'Me? You're the one
who——'

'Just look at this mess.' He pulled a white handkerchief from his breast pocket and rubbed at the spots on
his tie. 'You've ruined my tie.'

She stared at him while she brushed at the fine silk of her jacket. It was wrecked, she thought unhappily, absolutely wrecked. What was a tie when compared to a suit?

'And I'm going to smell like a bottle of Scotch for the rest of the afternoon.'

Olivia's mouth narrowed. 'Next time,' she snapped, 'stick to club soda. If nothing else, it might improve your disposition.'

His head came up. 'Really?' he said, and for the first time he looked straight at her.

'Really,' she started to say in a frigid tone, but the word stuck in her throat. The anger was draining from his face, leaving in its place a slow, easy smile. Olivia caught her breath. My God, she thought foolishly, what a handsome man.

'Hell,' he said pleasantly, 'accidents happen.'

She swallowed. 'Yes. I—I guess they do.'

Not just handsome. Wealthy. She knew the type too well. She could see it in the expensively tailored suit, hear it in the way he spoke.

She flushed as she realised how he was looking at her, his gaze moving slowly, lingering on the quick rise and fall of her breasts. His smile tilted.

'Here.' The hand that held the handkerchief lifted towards her bosom. 'Let me——'

'No.' Olivia stepped back quickly. 'I'll take care of it,' she said coldly.

'*Madame*? Sir? Is there a problem?'

She spun around. The head waiter was standing beside them, a worried frown on his face.

The man smiled. 'No problem at all.'

The head waiter's glance went from Olivia's jacket to the man's tie. 'May I get either of you something? A clean cloth, perhaps, or——?'

'A table,' the man said.

He took Olivia's elbow, his fingers curling around it very lightly, far too lightly for her to feel as if his touch had scorched her skin, but that was exactly how she felt. She pulled away sharply.

'I'm meeting someone,' she said to the head waiter.

He laughed softly. 'So was I. But it's not too late to change our plans, is it?'

'In fact,' she said, ignoring him, 'she might be here already. Her name is——'

'It's your name I'm interested in,' the man murmured. 'If you won't have lunch with me, at least give me your name and phone number.'

The head waiter cleared his throat. 'Perhaps I should return in a few minutes.'

'No.' Olivia shook her head. 'No, please. I'd like to be shown to my table, whether my friend is here or not.'

'Certainly, *madame*.'

'Say goodbye, at least,' the amused masculine voice beside her whispered as she marched off after the head waiter, but she didn't answer. She didn't take an easy breath, either, not until they'd safely left the bar behind.

'The reservation is in the name of Ria Bascomb,' she said.

The head waiter bowed his head. 'Of course. Just follow me, please.'

Olivia sighed. Ria was here already, then. Well, that figured. The day was rapidly going downhill. Just look at how badly she'd dealt with what had been, after all, nothing but an innocent flirtation. But the stranger had dredged up memories with his easy assumption that she'd find him irresistible.

'Here you are, *madame*.'

'Thank you. I . . .' Olivia blinked. There was someone in the booth waiting for her, all right, but it wasn't Ria. It was, instead, a white-haired man with a handsome, ruddy face who was already smiling and rising to his feet.

'Excuse me,' she said, turning to the head waiter. 'I'm afraid there's been a mistake.'

The white-haired man smiled and waved his hand in dismissal. 'That's all right, Geoffrey. Miss Harris is at the right table.'

'I'm sorry,' she said slowly, 'but I don't...' Her voice trailed away. She'd been going to say she didn't know this man, but she did. His face was familiar, as was his voice. Where had she seen him before?

'Charles Wright,' he said, as if he'd read her thoughts. 'We met several months ago. I came into the shop where you work to enquire about draperies for my apartment.'

'And you ended up having us redecorate the entire flat.' Olivia smiled and took the hand he held out to her. 'Of course, Mr Wright. Forgive me for not recognising you.'

'That's quite all right, Miss Harris.' Wright's smile grew warmer. 'I wouldn't expect such a beautiful young woman to remember the name and face of an old fogey like me.'

'Oh, but you're not an old fogey,' Olivia said automatically. 'I just—well, it's the lighting in here. And then...' She frowned as she withdrew her hand from his. 'I'm afraid there's been an error, Mr Wright. I'm meeting a friend for lunch——'

'Ria Bascomb.'

Her eyebrows rose. 'Yes. Yes, that's right. But how did you know?'

'Ria didn't tell you that she'd asked me to join you?' Wright sighed. 'Ah, well, she said she was going to keep it a secret till the last, and I see that she did.'

Olivia's frown deepened. 'Do you and Ria know each other?'

She had, apparently, made a marvellous joke. Wright laughed with delight.

'You might say that. In fact, we met at the shop where you work. I was in to approve the final sketches for my *pied à terre*, and Ria dropped by to say hello. You introduced us.'

'Did I?' Olivia smiled tentatively. 'Yes, now that you mention it, I think I do remember. But that still doesn't explain——'

'Please, Miss Harris, won't you sit down and have something to drink? Ria will be here soon, I assure you.'

Olivia hesitated for a few seconds, and then she shrugged her shoulders and slipped on to the cushioned seat opposite Wright while her brain whirred and tried to make sense out of what was happening. Alice at the Tea Party, she thought, and she cleared her throat.

'I must admit,' she said lightly, 'I'm not sorry she's not here yet. I'm always the one who's late, and I promised her I'd be on time today.' There was a silence, and she cleared her throat again. 'Well. I hope you're enjoying your flat, Mr Wright.'

'Charles.' His mouth curled up in a smile. 'Surely the woman who decorated my flat so beautifully knows me well enough to call me by my given name.'

Olivia gave him a little smile. 'Has it all worked out, then? As I recall, you were concerned that the colour we used in your living-room might become boring.'

Wright laughed. 'Actually, I wasn't in it often enough to notice. No, I'm just teasing you.' He smiled as he signalled the waiter. 'Everyone complimented me on the décor. We told them all it was done by the charming Miss Olivia Harris.'

Olivia flushed. 'Thank you, but I suspect my boss would rather you gave credit to Interiors by Pierre.'

'Nonsense.' Wright shrugged his elegantly clad shoulders. 'We both know that you're the creative one in that shop.'

'That's very kind, but——'

'What will you have to drink? White wine? Red? Perhaps something more substantial?'

Olivia hesitated. 'Perrier would be just fine, thank you.'

Wright made a face. 'On your birthday? Whatever are you thinking of?'

She stared at him. 'You know that it's my birthday?'

'A bottle of *Perrier-Jouet brut*,' he said to the waiter, and then he leaned forward towards Olivia. 'Yours, and Ria's. Of course I know. That's the reason I'm here.'

'To celebrate Ria's birthday?'

Wright chuckled softly. 'Or perhaps it's more accurate to say I'm here to celebrate yours.'

Olivia's head came up. 'Mr Wright——'

'Charles.'

'Look, I don't mean to seem rude, but I was expecting to meet my friend for lunch. Instead, I find you waiting for me, and, while you seem to know a great deal about me, I don't know anything at all about you.'

'But you do, my dear. You know that I'm a friend of Ria's, that I'm one of your most satisfied clients...' He sighed. 'I told Ria she was the one to explain this, but she insisted it should be me.'

'Explain what?' Olivia said, her expression cautious.

He sighed again. 'Ria and I were talking one day. About investment opportunities. She knows I'm always looking for——' He broke off as the *sommelier* appeared with a bottle of chilled champagne. Once it was opened and poured, Wright leaned across the table. 'Ria understands my fascination with investing in small businesses, so when she explained how profitable a small interior decorating studio could be...'

Olivia's breath caught with excitement. Was this what Ria had been hinting at? Had she found someone with the money to open a shop but not the knowledge? Was Wright asking her to manage such a place for him?

It was almost too good to be true. She moistened her lips with the tip of her tongue.

'Mr Wright—Charles—let me be sure I understand. Are you asking me to manage a shop for you?'

And it *was* too good to be true, she thought as he shook his head.

'No.'

Olivia nodded. 'Sorry.' She gave him a shaky smile. 'I thought I must have misunderstood, but for a minute there I could have sworn you said you were going into the interior decorating business.'

'*You're* going into the decorating business.' Wright lifted his glass and smiled at her over its rim. 'I'm just supplying the capital.'

She really was losing her mind, Olivia thought as the man opposite her laughed at the befuddled look that spread across her face.

'It's really very simple,' he said. 'I told you, I got lots of compliments on my flat, enough so it was very easy to sell.'

'You sold it? But we just finished re-doing it.'

He nodded. 'Yes. But my needs changed, Olivia. I needed something a bit quieter, with greater privacy.' He leaned forward. 'I didn't ask you to decorate the new place because—because it had just been done.'

'That's all right,' Olivia said, puzzled. 'You don't have to explain.'

'The point is, each time someone said how handsome the flat was, Ria would think of all the clients you were losing by not having a studio of your own.' Wright chuckled. 'So I wasn't all that surprised when she came up with this idea.'

Olivia put down her glass of wine very carefully. 'What idea?'

'She told me you'd tried to get a loan from the bank but they'd turned you down. That's right, isn't it?'

'I tried to get loans from several banks,' Olivia said. Her voice was thready; she cleared her throat and tried again. 'I don't see——'

'Ria suggested I finance your endeavour.'

Olivia stared at him. 'What?'

'I told you, I'm always looking for small investments. Well, why not invest in an interior design studio? Ria said, and I thought, Why not?'

A small investment, Olivia thought giddily. Yes, the money she needed would be that, to someone like Charles Wright. A practical gift, Ria had said. A pragmatic one. A downright sensible one...

'So I asked my attorneys to check things out, and they came up with some figures. Just preliminary ones, naturally, until they've had some input from you.'

The man was serious! Olivia stared at him across the table. A studio of her very own, one where she would make the decisions, not Pierre; one where she would take the credit, not Pierre; one where the decisions and the designs would all be hers.

But it was crazy. Insane. Heaven only knew how Ria had convinced Charles Wright to make such a generous offer. She couldn't accept it, of course; she...

'...And if you're thinking this is an act of lunacy that Ria talked me into...'

She gave a nervous laugh. 'I was thinking something like that,' she admitted.

'Well, I assure you, it isn't. Over the years, I've put money into a dry-cleaning shop, a video chain, even a haircutting establishment.' He smiled. 'Why not a decorating shop? My accountants tell me that the changing economy has altered people's habits. They're spending money on re-doing, rather than on starting afresh.'

'Yes, but—but you barely know me...'

'I know your work, and Ria vouches for you. That's good enough. And it is a loan, Olivia, understand that, with interest payments and a monthly due date and all the rest.' He smiled. 'My accountants, and the tax people, wouldn't have it any other way.'

Olivia blew out her breath. 'I—I don't know what to say,' she whispered.

Wright laughed. 'An astute businesswoman would simply say yes.'

She stared at him. 'How did you get started?' she'd asked Pierre once, and he'd shrugged his elegantly clad shoulders and answered with more honesty than she'd expected. 'A loan from a wealthy friend,' he'd said. 'Without her, I'd probably still be painting peonies on silk scarves.'

Wright drew a cheque from his breast pocket and pushed it across the table. 'Have a look at this. My people said it would get you started, but if it's not right, say so. I'd want to see you capitalised properly. If we want the right clientele to find you, we have to set you up in the right location and with the right sort of ambience.'

The cheque was for an amount that made Olivia's head spin. She stared at it, then at Wright.

'I—I don't know,' she said slowly. 'What if I fail?' She pushed the cheque back towards him, the light glinting off her diamond and gold watch. He stopped the cheque's progress by covering her hand with his.

'Ria and I have every confidence in you.'

She stared at him blankly. 'Mr Wright...'

'Charles.' He grinned engagingly. 'Surely we're on a first-name basis now.'

'Charles,' she said slowly, and then she fell silent. Ria, she thought, I'm going to break your neck. I'm going to hug you to death. I'm going to—I'm going to get up any minute and dance and shout and throw my arms around that stuffy head waiter...

'Are the funds sufficient, then?'

She nodded. 'Oh, yes, Charles. It's more than enough. It's just that I—I don't know if I can accept it. I'd feel funny, letting you give me such an enormous amount of money.'

'What a lovely sentiment. She almost sounds as if she means it.'

The voice was male, the tone soft. But there was no mistaking the coldness of it, nor the undisguised contempt. And there was certainly no mistaking its familiarity.

It was the man who'd bumped into her only moments ago. Olivia drew herself up and gave him a cold stare.

'You're not welcome here,' she began, but then she stopped. The stranger wasn't looking at her at all, he was looking at Charles—and Charles was looking back at him, his ruddy face gone pale as a sheet.

'How nice to see you again, Charles,' he said, but she knew that wasn't what he meant at all. Charles knew it, too; his hand, still clutching hers over the cheque, tightened until his grip was almost painful.

Olivia cleared her throat. 'Do you—do you know this man, Charles?'

The man laughed. 'Do you know me, Charles?' he said, his voice cruelly mimicking hers.

'Edward.' Charles's voice was a little breathless. 'This is a surprise.'

Edward gave a sharp laugh. 'Yes. I can imagine.'

Olivia frowned. Something was going on here, something unpleasant, but what? The stranger was staring at her luncheon companion. She couldn't see his eyes clearly—they were blue or black, it was hard to be certain which—but it was obvious that they were icy with what could only be described as unbridled hatred.

A little shudder rocketed through her. Clearing her throat, she began rising to her feet.

'I'll just go to the ladies' room so you gentlemen can——'

'No.' Charles's fingers clasped hers more tightly, and Olivia winced as she fell back into her seat. 'No,' he repeated. 'Edward's not—he's not staying. Are you, Edward?'

The other man smiled, although Olivia wasn't quite sure that was the correct word to describe the way his lips drew back over his teeth.

'I've a lunch with some business associates,' he said softly. His gaze swept across the table, where Olivia's hand, still clutching the cheque, lay trapped by Charles's. The terrible smile came again, swift and chill, and his eyes lifted to Olivia's. 'You had an appointment, you said. But I'd no idea who the lucky man was.'

Charles swallowed convulsively. 'Do you—do you know Miss Harris, Edward?'

The man's lips drew back from his teeth. 'Not half as well as you do,' he said.

'Now, wait just a minute,' Olivia began, and Charles's fingers squeezed hers again.

'Miss Harris and I were just——'

'Don't tell me.' The stranger's gaze drifted with slow insolence from Olivia's face to her breasts. She felt a rush of crimson suffuse her cheeks; when his gaze finally met hers again, he laughed softly, as if he and she were sharing some awful joke. 'You were discussing business,' he said. 'Any man with half a brain could figure that out.'

The words were innocent, but the insult had been blatant none the less. Olivia snatched her hand from Wright's and got to her feet. She forced herself to look straight at the man blocking her way.

'Excuse me,' she said coldly.

'Don't leave on my account, darling. I'm sure you and Charles still have lots of "business" to discuss.'

'Would you please step aside?'

'So well-mannered.' His teeth flashed in that awful smile again. 'And so lovely. I must admit, Charles, your taste is impeccable.'

'Just who in hell do you think you are?' Olivia demanded in quiet fury.

'Why don't you tell her, Charles?' the man said softly, his eyes never leaving Olivia's face.

'Edward.' Charles's voice was low and tense. 'You've made an error. I told you, Miss Harris is——'

'A business associate. Of course.' He reached out suddenly and caught hold of Olivia's arm. His hand curved tightly around it, the fingers long and tanned against the green silk. 'That's a lovely bauble, darling.' She grimaced as he twisted her wrist upwards. Light gleamed on Ria's last birthday gift, the diamond and gold watch.

'You must be pretty good to have gotten such a bonus from old Charlie.'

Olivia twisted her hand free of his. 'Let go of me!' she demanded, her voice thrumming with barely suppressed rage. 'Let go, or I'll...'

'You'll what?' he asked, so softly that only she could hear him. 'Struggle? Fight me?' He shifted his weight so that they stood as close together as if they were lovers. His smile grew lazy, almost sensual; she could feel the heat coming off his taut body. 'Go on,' he said quietly, 'why don't you try it?'

Her eyes narrowed with anger, and almost of its own volition her hand flashed up to strike his face, but he caught her wrist effortlessly and held it immobile in a strong, harsh grasp. The smile fled, and his eyes changed from cold pools of blue light to black winter ice.

'Enjoy your lunch, Miss Harris,' he said, and before she could collect herself enough to think of a response he'd turned on his heel and marched away.

'Olivia. Olivia!' She blinked and swung towards the banquette. Charles Wright was motioning to her. Tiny beads of sweat dotted his forehead. 'Sit down, Olivia,' he hissed. 'Everyone's looking at us.'

But he was wrong. The dimness of the lighting and the location of the booth had protected them; no one was looking at them at all.

Leave, she told herself, just head for the door and keep on going...but her legs felt like rubber. She needed to sit down before she fell down, and she collapsed into her seat, reached for her glass of champagne, and drained it dry.

'I'm sorry,' Charles said miserably. 'I'm really sorry, Olivia.'

Olivia shook her head. 'Who was that man?' she whispered.

'Someone who thinks he owns the world,' he said grimly.

There was anger and determination in his voice now, but where had those emotions been while their unwelcome visitor had loomed over them? That bastard! The things he'd said to her—the things he'd implied . . .

She closed her eyes and leaned her head back against the cushioned banquette. Some birthday this had turned out to be! A stranger for a luncheon companion instead of Ria, an offer to start her own business—even though accepting the money now was surely out of the question—and an encounter with a—a madman, an absolute madman . . .

'Livvie!' The scent of Poison filled the air. Olivia's eyes flew open as Ria Bascomb dropped into the booth beside her in a flurry of sable and silk. 'Oh, Livvie, can you ever forgive me?' She pressed her cheek to Olivia's and smiled at Charles. 'Hello, Charlie. Did you two have a nice chat?'

'Ria,' Charles said. 'Thank God you've finally arrived. We just——'

'Well? Did you tell her?' Ria peeled off her kidskin gloves and tossed them on the table. 'Well, Livvie, what do you think? I wanted you to hear the details from Charlie, so you'd understand it wasn't just me trying to give you a . . .' Her voice trailed off and she frowned. 'What's wrong here? I thought you two would have become the best of friends by now. Livvie, don't tell me you're angry because of Charlie's offer?'

Charles leaned forward. 'Edward just paid us a visit,' he said tightly.

Ria's head came up. 'Edward? Good lord, Charles. What was he doing here?'

'Making trouble. That's all he ever does, isn't it?'

'Yes, but Edward—here? What did he say?'

'He said a lot of awful things—most of them directed at me.' Olivia's voice trembled. 'And I've no idea why. Who in God's name is he?'

Ria and Charles looked at each other, and then they both spoke at once.

'Edward is——'

'Edward's——'

Charles fell silent, and Ria cleared her throat. 'Edward is—he's a member of Charles's family. He—he resents Charles's wealth, Livvie, oh, it's all very complicated. Byzantine, you might say. But the bottom line is that he thinks he should have control of the family funds—which he'd squander, of course. And he never misses the chance to insult Charles if he can.'

Olivia puffed out her breath. 'Well, he's very good at it, I must say.' She gave a shaky little laugh. 'He made me feel as if—as if...' Her eyes lifted to Ria's. 'But he did make me realise one thing. I can't accept your offer.'

'My offer?'

'Well, Charles's offer. I do thank you, Ria, it was quite the nicest birthday ever, but——' Olivia took a breath. 'It really was very generous, but it's out of the question.'

Ria propped her elbows on the table and steepled her fingers beneath her chin.

'Why?'

'Well, because it just is. I mean, Charles doesn't know anything about the decorating business...'

'He's not supposed to. You're the decorator, remember?'

'And—and who knows if I can make a go of my own studio? I've only been out of school four years.'

'Nonsense. That fat jerk Pierre hasn't lifted a pencil to a sketchpad since he made you his assistant and everybody knows it. What else?'

'Well...' Olivia flushed. 'I just wouldn't feel right taking so much money from a stranger.'

'Edward made some insinuations,' Charles said tightly.

Ria's brows rose. 'Did he?'

'Yes,' Olivia said. 'Of course,' she added quickly, 'I know they were lies. I mean, Charles never even suggested...'

'He'd better not have.' Ria leaned across the table and reached for Charles's hand while Olivia stared in surprise. 'Charlies and I have become very close, Livvie,' she said softly. 'Did he tell you?'

'No.' Olivia swallowed hard. 'No, he didn't.'

'Well, it's true.'

'I see,' Olivia said, although she didn't. Ria and Charles? There had to be thirty years separating them, at least. 'Well then, why would this Edward person have acted as if he thought Charles and I were—as if he thought we were...?'

'Edward is—he's actually related to Charles's wife. And Charles is separated from her.' Ria flushed when Olivia looked at her. 'Don't look like that, Livvie. This is the twentieth century. Besides, it happened before we met.'

'I—I'm just surprised, Ria,' Olivia said slowly. 'You never said...'

'Well, we don't talk much any more, do we?' Ria said defensively. 'Anyway, Edward doesn't really care about our situation.' Her pretty face set in grim lines. 'I told you, all he wants is to get his hands on Charles's money— as if what he already has weren't enough. And he's got an attitude about women that went out with the cavemen.'

Olivia's mouth thinned. 'Yes.' Her fingers went to her wrist and rubbed lightly over the bruised flesh. 'I'll agree with that.'

'Look, what can I tell you? Edward Archer was born with a silver spoon in his mouth.' Ria made a face. 'You know the type, Livvie. He resents anybody who doesn't fit the mould.'

Yes, she knew the type. She knew it all too well. She'd grown up around boys like that, ones who came from families with old names and older money, who saw girls like her as toys. They were boys who grew into men with the same attitude.

Had Edward Archer seen right through all the layers added to herself over the years, the clothes, the sophistication, the quietly flawless make-up? Olivia's mouth narrowed. Was that why he'd thought he would come on to her when they'd first bumped into each other, why he could insult her, why he'd misunderstood her relationship with Charles? Did she still somehow bear the mark that set her apart, that showed that she was not 'to the manor born'?

'Livvie, you're not going to be foolish enough to let someone like that stop you from accepting Charles's loan and changing your life, are you?' Ria took Olivia's hand in hers. 'Are you, Livvie?'

Olivia looked at her friend. Ria's smile was open and warm; Charles was looking at her with love shining in his eyes, and she thought suddenly of the way Edward Archer had looked at her, as if she were dirt beneath his feet.

'Certainly not,' she said without any more hesitation, and in that instant sealed her fate.

CHAPTER TWO

DAMN Edward Archer to hell! She barely knew the man with eyes like winter ice, and yet he'd managed to reduce her, a self-assured woman, to the shy, awkward girl she'd been years ago.

The knowledge, lodged like a stone in her breast, was enough to steal some of the pleasure from Ria's 'gift'. But as the days passed, Olivia was too busy to dwell on anything as insignificant as an encounter with a rude bully.

There were meetings with lawyers and with accountants, with real estate agents and painters and plasterers, and one memorable half-hour with Monsieur Pierre during which he first accused her of being an untalented, ungrateful upstart—and then all but got on his knees and begged her to accept a huge rise and stay on in his employ.

It was that acknowledgement of her worth that convinced her that leaving Interiors by Pierre and opening her own shop was the right thing to do.

It all came together quickly. Olivia fell in love with a narrow, four-storey town house on a tree-lined Manhattan street. She took a deep breath, put down a chunk of Charles's loan, and the place was hers. The top floor became a small but comfortable flat that put an end to years of living in a cramped bed-sitter. The lower three levels were transformed into a design studio and showrooms that had, until now, only been a dream.

And that was what she named her shop: Olivia's Dream.

She designed every square inch of it herself, so that it wasn't only the showroom that had flash and dash, which was the way it had been at Pierre's. He had been big on dazzling the customers, but he hadn't cared a damn for his designers.

'Life in the salt mines,' Dulcie Chambers, who'd worked with Olivia, had said of their cramped, rather grim studio. They'd both tried to make the place more cheerful, but potted geraniums and framed prints had not been able to do the impossible.

'When I have my own place,' Dulcie had said wistfully, 'it'll be a million feet square, with wall-to-wall windows and hundred-foot ceilings.'

Olivia had smiled archly. 'When I have mine,' she'd said, 'it'll be a *zillion* feet square, with thousand-foot ceilings. I won't have any walls at all, I'll just have glass, glass, and more glass. How's that sound?'

'Like heaven,' the other girl had sighed—and now, thanks to Ria and Charles, it had all come true.

Well, perhaps not quite all, Olivia thought, smiling a little as she looked up from her drafting table. The room on the second floor in which she and Dulcie worked now—the other girl had leaped at Olivia's job offer—was a bit shy of being a zillion feet square and a thousand feet high. But it was big and bright and filled with cheerful colours, and, if it wasn't a zillion square feet, it was as close to it as the architect could manage.

'Are you happy, Livvie?' Ria had asked just yesterday, when the two friends had met at the Plaza for drinks after Olivia's Dream had closed for the day.

Olivia had smiled. 'Do you really need to ask?' she'd said, and Ria had beamed with delight.

And she was happy, Olivia thought as she picked up her sketch-pad, pushed back her stool, and walked slowly to the window. Most of the time—and, if there were occasional shadows and misgivings, she could hardly mention them to Ria.

Charles had been a perfect gentleman in the weeks since he'd offered to back her financially. He'd never given her a moment's reason to regret her decision to accept his loan. Nevertheless, she couldn't escape the feeling that the Charles she did business with and the Charles who was courting Ria were in some ways different men. And why was Ria so intent on keeping her relationship with him a secret?

Because Charles's lawyers had advised it, until his divorce was final, Ria said. And then, she'd added with a sigh, and then there were her parents.

'You know how they are, Livvie.'

Olivia did, all too well. The Bascombs had always treated her pleasantly, but they'd never quite let her forget that she was their housekeeper's ward and living in their house on sufferance.

'You mean,' she'd said after a moment, 'that they're a bit conservative.'

Ria had sighed. 'Stuffy and uptight's a better way to describe it. If I tell them about Charles, they'll go crazy. They'll say he's too old for me, they'll be horrified that he's still married . . .'

'Maybe you ought to think about those things, too,' Olivia had said gently.

'Come on, Livvie, you've come to know him. Why, he's got more energy than some men half his age. As for his marriage—I've told you, it's been unhappy for years.'

'Still, all this—this subterfuge is—is——'

'—is necessary,' Ria had said firmly. 'Until his divorce is final, anyway, and then we'll go to Vegas and get married and then present my parents with a—what do you call it?—a *fait accompli*.'

It sounded more like sneaking around to Olivia, but she'd known better than to put Ria on the defensive.

'I just don't want to see you get hurt,' she'd said instead, and Ria had smiled as she reached across the table and took hold of Olivia's hand.

'I know,' she'd whispered. 'Oh, Livvie, I'm so glad we're close again,' she'd said. 'I've missed you.'

They weren't close again, not really, but Olivia hadn't the heart to say it to the girl who'd once been as much sister as best friend. Instead, she'd smiled and grasped Ria's hand tightly.

'Me, too,' she'd said, and that had ended the conversation.

And then there was Edward Archer. Olivia caught her bottom lip between her teeth. It was crazy, but the ugly run-in with him had never been far from her thoughts, as if her mind had only been waiting for her to have time to think about something other than architectural plans and structural sketches to relive those awful moments in the restaurant.

And that was ridiculous. The incident had occurred almost a month ago, and she hadn't seen him since.

Why, then, was she remembering it? Without warning, there'd be the image of him, standing close to her. She'd see the tall, leanly muscled body, the eyes that had danced with sexual appraisal when he'd tried to pick her up and had later damned her with sexual contempt. Edward Archer had given her a look that had clearly said, If I wanted you, I could have you, I could subdue you and make you cry your need for me into the darkness...

Her body flooded with the heat of humiliation, and Olivia leaned her forehead against the cool window-pane.

Years ago, she'd stepped off a kerb on a rainy night into the path of a sports car just as the light went green. She'd heard the angry roar of the engine as it revved— and then, almost too late, the driver had seen her and hadn't released the clutch pedal. But that frightening sense of something powerful, something held under taut control just waiting to be unleashed, had left a lasting impact.

Confronting Edward Archer had been like that. Despite the elegant cut of his suit and the scent of expensive cologne, there'd been an animal edge to him. Instinct warned her he'd been holding himself in tight control. It was as if she'd glimpsed the expert assassin that lurked just beneath the civilised exterior of any well-groomed house cat. It had been in the feel of his hand clamping down on her arm, in the hint of dark stubble barely visible on skin tautly drawn over the hard bones in his face.

She caught her breath. What would it feel like, that shadowy stubble, moving lightly against a woman's tender flesh? Rough, slightly abrasive, as his mouth traced a path down her throat, across her shoulders, across her breasts...

'Olivia?' The sketch-pad fell from her hands as she spun around. Dulcie stood in the open doorway, her fair hair a bright nimbus around her freckled face. 'I'm sorry,' she said, 'I didn't mean to startle you.'

Olivia swallowed. 'That's OK. I was—I—I was trying to come up with a design for those draperies we've been...' Her voice faded as she bent and picked up the pad. 'And getting nowhere,' she said briskly. 'Is it my turn to be salesgirl?'

'No, I'm still the lucky one.' Dulcie's brows rose. 'Actually, someone's asking for you.'

'A customer?' Olivia said. All thoughts of Edward Archer faded away at the prospect. Each new order was still something of an event.

'No. I don't think so.'

'Ah, well.' Olivia sighed dramatically. 'I wonder what permit I'm missing this time, although heaven only knows what could possibly be left. Department of Health, Department of Taxation, Department of Labour... what more could any man want of me?'

'A great deal—unless he were a damned fool.'

Olivia's heartbeat stuttered. 'Olivia?' Dulcie said, but Olivia was already twisting towards the sound of that softly insinuating voice.

Edward Archer stood lounging in the studio's open doorway, his navy suit jacket open over a cream shirt and dark silk tie, his hands tucked casually into the pockets of his trousers so that the fabric drew tautly across his thighs. He smiled when he saw Olivia's eyes widen in shock, his mouth tilting up at one corner to give an even more suggestive twist to his words.

Olivia didn't hesitate. 'How dare you come here?'

His smile became a lazy grin. 'That's a hell of a way to greet a client.' His gaze swept over her with slow insolence, moving down the beige linen suit she'd designed herself to the Charles Jourdan pumps picked up on sale last spring, returning at last to her face. 'Or has old Charlie supplied you with all the "clients" a girl could possibly handle?'

Olivia's face coloured. He was doing it again, here on her own territory.

'I wouldn't count on old Charlie for very much, Olivia.' He stepped away from the door-frame, moved into the room, and strolled the length of it, pausing every few feet to glance at the sketches tacked on the walls. 'Actually,' he said after a moment, his voice very soft, almost silken, 'I wouldn't count on old Charlie at all, if I were you.'

Damn the man! Olivia gave herself a mental shake, then drew herself up. 'You're not welcome here, Mr Archer,' she said in a cold voice.

It was as if she hadn't spoken. He didn't even glance at her. Instead, he paused at the windows that looked down on the town house's tiny garden.

'Nice. Very nice.' He swung towards her and gave her a smile that was all even white teeth. 'Who'd have thought such a transparent ploy would work, Olivia? Telling old Charlie you couldn't accept whatever he was offering that day, convincing him you didn't want his money——'

'Get out!' She took a step forward. 'Do you hear me, Mr Archer? You get out of my office this minute!'

'I guess he upped the ante, hmm?' Archer leaned back against the window ledge and folded his arms across his chest. 'Hell, Charlie always was an old fool for...' His eyes moved over her again, very slowly and very deliberately, and she had to fight against the terrible desire to cover herself with her hands. 'Although this time I can almost understand why.'

Dulcie cleared her throat. 'Olivia? Shall I—shall I do something?' She looked from Edward Archer to her employer. 'I mean, do you want me to—to call somebody, or—or...?'

'You can show this—this "gentleman" out, Dulcie.'

Archer's smile faded. 'I'm not leaving.'

Dulcie shifted closer to Olivia. 'What do you want me to do?' she whispered.

Edward Archer answered before Olivia could speak. 'She wants you to go out and close the door after you,' he said softly. His eyes locked with Olivia's. 'Isn't that right, Miss Harris?'

'No,' Olivia said quickly, almost breathlessly. 'Don't—don't go, Dulcie.'

Hearing the pathetic tremor in her own voice made her flinch. How dared he do this to her? She belonged here, not he. It was he who was the outsider.

The realisation gave her strength.

'If you have something to say to me, Mr Archer,' she said coolly, 'you'd better get to it.'

'Tell her to go.' He jerked his head towards Dulcie, who was still gaping. He was all business now; something about the look in his eyes and the set to his mouth sent a chill up Olivia's spine. 'You and I have things to discuss, Miss Harris. I suggest we deal with them in private.'

'Olivia? Should I—should I call the cops?'

Edward Archer, in the hands of the police! Oh, but the thought was tempting! But calling them would be a foolish indulgence, and Olivia knew it. Olivia's Dream was on a quiet street; she'd spent a small fortune on discreet advertisements in *The Times* and a handful of pricey magazines, but one visit from a police car with its lights flashing and its siren wailing would bring down the kind of publicity her business might never live down.

Besides, every instinct warned that she should hear him out. There was a grim determination about him now; whatever had brought him here would have to be dealt with.

'No, Dulcie,' she said quietly, 'that won't be necessary. You just go on down to the showroom.' It was hard to smile, but she managed. 'We don't want to miss any clients, do we?'

The girl's mouth tightened. 'I'm going to stay right outside the door,' she said with a meaningful glower in Edward's direction. 'You call and I'll come running.'

Olivia waited until the door swung shut. She looked down at her watch and then at Edward Archer.

'You have one minute,' she said coldly.

A muscle twitched in his jaw. 'This is going to take a hell of a lot longer than that.'

'One minute, Mr Archer. And so far, you've wasted almost five seconds.'

'You've got your act together since we last met.' She looked up. He was watching her narrowly, his eyes cool and assessing. 'The Lady of the Manor thing, I mean. Very nicely done. I'm impressed.'

'Nine seconds gone, Mr Archer.'

His lips drew back from his teeth. 'And then what? Will you throw me out?'

'Thirty-nine seconds left, and counting down,' she said as she walked to her corner desk. She bent and riffled through the papers strewn across it. What did he want? Damn it all, *what did he want*?

'Because we both know you won't be able to do that.' She went very still as she felt him come up behind her. His breath ruffled her hair. 'I can overpower you,' he said softly. 'I can do whatever I want with you, Olivia, and we both know it.'

She felt her heart begin to race. One one thousand, she thought, two one thousand, three...

When she was certain she could face him without trembling, she turned around.

'Does trying to intimidate me make you feel good?' she asked quietly.

His mouth twisted. 'You know damned well that isn't what I was doing.'

'Because if that's how you get your kicks, Mr Archer...'

She caught her breath as his hands clasped her shoulders. His fingers were hard on her flesh; she felt their touch in the marrow of her bones. His eyes swept over her face and fastened on her mouth.

'Have you thought about me?' he asked.

'No,' she said quickly. Too quickly; even she knew that.

His hand rose and lightly encircled the nape of her neck, the fingers sifting into the loose knot of silken hair pinned at the back of her head. She felt strands of it fall free and drift to her shoulders.

'I've been thinking about you, Olivia.'

His voice was soft, like the caress of his fingers against her skin. She felt herself sway a little, just a little, as if his stroking fingers were mesmerising her.

'Actually,' she said, 'I have thought about you, Mr Archer. I've had nightmares that you might turn up in my life again and be even more rude than you were the last time.'

He smiled. 'I think about you at night, when I lie in my bed.' His voice grew soft and rough with promise. 'I imagine you naked, in my arms, your hair spread like a dark cloud across my pillow.'

Her heart gave an unsteady thump as she tried to break away from him. 'You have no right——'

'I remember the smell of you, and I wonder what you taste like.' She gasped as he drew her closer. 'You wonder too, Olivia. I can see it in your eyes, feel it in the way your body heats under my hand.'

'You're crazy,' she said. Her voice was cool, so cool. But her skin felt hot and flushed.

'Sometimes I can almost hear you cry out my name as I touch you.'

A picture flashed into her mind. She saw herself in his arms, trembling under his caresses, straining towards him in the heat of desire, and an emotion she could not identify raced through her blood.

'Never,' she hissed, 'not in the next million years. Not if you were the last...'

His hands fell away from her so suddenly that she fell back against the desk.

'Be careful what you say, darling.' His voice had gone as cold as his eyes. 'You can never tell when you may just need the last man on earth.'

Olivia raised her hands to the back of her head. They shook as she tried to smooth back her hair and re-pin it.

'I'd never need anything from you,' she said in a shaky voice. 'Not as long as I have——'

'Sweet old Charlie.' An ugly smile twisted across his mouth. 'What a touching sentiment, Olivia.'

Not as long as I have two hands to work with, she'd been going to say. But why should she defend herself to Edward Archer? Her chin rose in defiance.

'It is, isn't it?' she said evenly. 'And now, Mr Archer, if you'll get to the reason you came here——'

'Sweet old Charlie is dead.'

The words were bluntly delivered. Olivia smiled uncertainly. 'What did you say?'

His eyes fixed on her face. 'You heard me, sweetheart. Charlie is dead. Kaput. He's history.'

Olivia blinked. Dead? No, that was impossible. She had seen Charles just last night, only for a few minutes when he'd come to pick Ria up at the Plaza after they'd had their drinks, and he'd been fine, just fine.

He laughed unpleasantly. 'Hell, at least old Charlie died a happy man.'

'Charles Wright?' she said stupidly.

Edward's lip curled. 'The late Charles Wright, my dear. How many other Charlies are there in your life? Maybe we ought to give 'em numbers. Charlie One, Charlie Two——'

Dead. Charles was dead. Ria, she thought, oh, Ria...

'Is he really dead?' she whispered.

'Dead as the dodo bird.'

Her eyes swept the hard, stony face before her. 'How can you talk that way? Don't you have any feelings?'

'Why should I? Nobody will mourn the bastard.'

Ria's face swam before her. 'Somebody will,' Olivia said softly, and she bent her head and put her hands to her eyes.

Edward Archer gave a muffled oath. 'If I live to be a thousand, I'll never understand what makes a woman cry!' His arms went around her, drawing her into a hard, unyielding embrace.

The shock drove the colour back into her face. Olivia slapped her hands against his chest.

'Let go of me!'

'I suppose a Victorian swoon comes next,' he said grimly as he stalked to the door.

'Don't be ridiculous. I——'

He threw the door open and stepped into the hall. Dulcie's startled gasp was sharp as a gunshot.

'Miss Harris isn't feeling well,' Edward said tightly. 'Where can she lie down?'

'Olivia? Olivia, what's he done to you? Do you want me to call the police now? Or an ambulance? Do you need an ambulance? Oh, Olivia...'

'I'm fine, Dulcie. Dammit, Mr Archer——'

'I asked you a question, girl!' Edward's voice was harsh. 'Where can Miss Harris lie down?'

Dulcie pointed a trembling finger. 'Upstairs,' she said. 'Olivia, shall I——?'

But he had already moved past Dulcie, shouldering her aside as he half carried Olivia up the narrow staircase that led to her flat.

'Would you please let go of me?' she demanded. 'You're making a fool of yourself, Mr Archer. I don't need your help. I don't *want* your help. Do you hear me?'

He ignored her protests, shouldered open the door, and stepped into her living-room.

'Where is your bedroom?' he demanded.

Not the bedroom. The last place she wanted this man was in her bedroom. Olivia's head might still be spinning, but she hadn't lost the power to think straight.

'The sofa's fine,' she said quickly.

He crossed the tiny room in a few strides and deposited her on the velvet-covered Empire sofa, then stood back and stared down at her, his face grim.

'Where do you keep your brandy?'

'Look, I don't need brandy.'

'Where is it?'

She threw up her hands. 'I don't have any.'

'Cognac, then. Whiskey. Where is it?'

'There's nothing in the house.'

'Hell, woman, you must have something on hand. What did Wright drink when he visited you?'

Her eyes fixed on his. There was absolutely no expression on his face, but the contempt in his voice was like a slap.

'He didn't,' she said coldly.

'Didn't drink?' One dark brow angled upwards. 'That's hard to believe. Old Charlie liked his liquor— almost as much as he liked his women.'

'He didn't visit me. And I resent you——'

'Don't give me that. He was in and out of this place.'

Olivia folded her arms across her chest. 'He visited the shop,' she said, even more coldly. 'Never my flat— not that it's any of your business.'

Edward's lips drew back from his teeth. 'Yeah. Right. Why would he, when he'd set up that nice little love nest for you over on Sutton Place?'

'What?'

'Come on, sweetheart, don't push your luck. You put on a pretty good act, I'll grant you that. But the show's over.' He strode across the room and into the efficiency kitchen. She could hear cabinet doors slamming and the tinkle of glass. 'Here,' he said, coming back to her with a glass of something red in his outstretched hand. 'Drink it down.'

'What is it?' Olivia's nose wrinkled as he pushed the glass under her nose. 'Ugh,' she said, 'I don't want that. It's——'

'It's cheap wine,' he said. 'Not Wright's taste at all, but it'll do the job. Go on, drink it.'

'It's cooking wine. And I told you, I don't need——'

'Drink,' he growled. His eyes flashed at her. 'Or must I hold your nose and pour it in?'

She stared at him, her eyes locking with his. Lord, how she despised this man! He would do it, she was certain, he'd hold her still and feed the noxious stuff into her unless she did as he demanded. He was strong. And intimidating. And very sure of himself, and she didn't want to take him on again, not now. All she wanted right this minute was to get Edward Archer out of her home so she could contact Ria and comfort her.

She reached out, snatched the glass from him and tossed down the bitter liquid. Her shoulders lifted, her throat convulsed, and she coughed explosively.

'There,' she gasped, 'are you satisfied now?'

He said nothing for a long moment, only watched her with that same empty expression on his face, his eyes hooded and unreadable. A little shudder went through her as she thought how he seemed to fill, even overwhelm, her small living-room.

He reached out and took the glass from her fingers. 'Hell, it's not every day you learn your benefactor's dead.'

Olivia's eyes narrowed. 'Charles Wright was a good man,' she said.

'Especially to you, sweetheart.' His teeth glinted in a quick grin. 'Hey, I can understand getting hysterical when you've suffered such a terrible loss.'

'I hate to spoil this moment of drama for you, Mr Archer,' she said coldly, 'but I was not hysterical.'

He shrugged lazily. 'Whatever you say, sweetheart.'

She rose to her feet. 'Goodbye, Mr Archer. I wish I could say it had been nice to see you again, but——'

He shook his head as he leaned back against the wall. 'I'm not leaving yet, Miss Harris,' he said, his formal tone mimicking hers.

'Yes, you are. We've nothing more to discuss.'

'We've plenty to discuss.' He cocked his head to the side and smiled again. 'For instance, what did you do to old Charlie to kill him?'

The blood rushed from her face. 'What?'

Edward laughed and held up his hand. 'Let me re-phrase that. What little tricks did you introduce him to last night, hmm?' His smile faded. 'It must have been something pretty cute to have done him in. Charlie was used to keeping fast company, but then I suppose a woman like you knows some things that can take a man as close to heaven as they do to hell.'

Olivia stared at him. 'Are you suggesting—are you trying to insinuate that I—that Charles and I were—that we were...?'

'I'm not insinuating anything.' Edward moved quickly; he was across the narrow room and standing next to her before she had time to react. 'I saw him, Olivia.' His voice was soft, silken, and filled with menace. 'I saw him in that big, silk-sheeted bed, I saw the imprint your head had left on the pillow beside his, I saw the bit of black lace you left tossed on the floor——'

'I don't have to listen to this nonsense,' Olivia began as she started past him.

Edward's hand closed tightly on her shoulder. 'It's too bad you weren't with him when he breathed his last, Miss Harris. After all, your lover——'

'Damn you!' Angry tears rose in her eyes as she twisted unsuccessfully in his grasp. 'He wasn't my lover!'

He pulled her to him. 'No?'

'No! He was——'

He was Ria's lover, she'd almost said. But no one knew that, and how could she name Ria without speaking to her first? Besides, neither she nor Ria owed this man any explanations. He was related to Charles's wife, Ria had said, and his only interest in Charles was in finding a way to get his hands on the family fortune. Well, she could see that for herself now. Edward Archer didn't give a damn about Charles's death. Whatever he was angry about, it wasn't because Charles Wright was no more.

'I don't owe you any explanations,' she said stiffly.

He laughed. 'No. I suppose you don't.' He stepped closer to her. 'But you might want to be a little nicer to me, baby, considering that you've lost your bread and butter.'

Olivia twisted against his hand. 'I don't have to be anything to you! You've no right to——'

'I have every right,' he said in a silken whisper. 'You'd better be a hell of a lot nicer to me.' She cried out as his arms went around her and he pulled her against the hardness of his long, powerful body. 'You're going to have bills to pay, sweetheart, and I control the estate.' He shifted her in his arms so that she was off balance; her weight fell against him and he smiled lazily at the feel of her body against his. 'You'll have to give up the flat in Sutton Place, of course.'

'You're insane! I don't have a——'

'But this place is pretty cosy. I might just let you keep it, and that pretty little design studio you play around in.'

'Get out!' she panted as she struggled to break free. 'Damn you to hell, Edward Archer, get——'

'Assuming you're as nice to me as you were to old Charlie,' he whispered, and then his mouth dropped to hers.

He was strong, as strong as she had known he would be. His arms imprisoned her, made her captive to the heat of his body. She cried out and tried to turn away from him.

'I can be as generous as he was,' he whispered against her mouth. He caught her head in his hands and held her so she couldn't get away. 'And I can make you happy in bed. We both know that.'

'You bastard!'

'Hell, we can make each other happy in bed,' he said thickly, and he bent to her and kissed her again.

It was the same way he'd kissed her the first time, it was an angry, overpowering kiss meant to remind her of who was in charge and of what he thought of her, and it sent rage rocketing through her.

'I hate you,' she whispered fiercely.

Edward went very still. 'Do you?' he whispered, and suddenly there was a subtle change in the way he was holding her. His arms were just as hard, his embrace as unyielding. His body burned against hers with the same urgency. But there was a strange kind of longing in the way he held her. His kiss changed, too. It gentled, asked instead of demanded, gave instead of took.

'Olivia,' he whispered, and with a little sob of defeat she lifted her arms and wound them tightly around his neck. She pressed herself to him, wanting the feel of him imprinted on her breasts, on her belly, wanting to feel the silken darkness of his hair under her caressing hand, to feel the heat of his mouth on hers.

He thrust her from him so suddenly that she almost fell. Her lashes lifted; she stared into his face, watching as his eyes went from sea-dark to ice.

'You see?' he said. 'It would be terrific.' His mouth twisted. 'But I'm not really sure I want to take another man's leavings.'

She didn't hesitate. Her hand came up and she hit him, hard, across the cheek. The crack of flesh against flesh was like the crack of lightning, and echoed through the small room. The look that flashed across Edward's face was ominous, but Olivia was past caring.

'You bastard,' she said in a choked whisper. 'You can't come into my home and treat me like this! Just who in hell do you think you are?'

His smile was slow and lazy, as if she'd finally asked him the only question worth an answer, and he seemed to take an eternity before he answered.

'I thought you knew,' he said softly. 'I'm Charles Wright's stepson.'

She stared at him in disbelief. 'You're not. You're a relative of his w...'

'I'm his stepson, Miss Harris. And I'm here to see to it that you don't keep one cent of what rightly belongs to my mother.'

'Your—your mother? But Charles was divorcing her.'

He laughed. 'Did he tell you that, too? Hell, it must have been his favourite bedtime tale.' The laughter fled his face. 'Listen and listen well, baby, because I'm only going to say this once before I let my attorneys do the talking.' One arm swept out in a gesture that took in everything: the flat, the floors beneath, and, Olivia knew, her very existence. 'You're not going to keep any of it Not this place, not the apartment leased in your name on Sutton Place——'

'What apartment?'

'You're going to lose it all, *Miss* Harris. My lawyers and I will see to that. So maybe you'd better shine up your shoes and go for a stroll. Pick a good spot, baby, and with any luck you might be able to find another sucker to replace good old Charlie.'

Olivia wrapped her arms around herself. 'Get out, she whispered, 'you—you...'

His teeth glinted in a quick smile. 'The lady's finally at a loss for words.' Turning, he reached for the doorknob. 'Not to worry, darling. Talk isn't what you're best at anyway.'

She took a step towards him. 'Get out of my house!'

'Enjoy it while you can.' He laughed softly. 'It won't be yours much longer.'

The door opened, then slammed shut, and Olivia was finally, mercifully, alone.

CHAPTER THREE

OLIVIA sat at her desk, her dark head illuminated by the light from the brass gooseneck lamp beside her. It was late, almost eight o'clock on a Wednesday evening, and the studio was quiet, the silence broken only by the whisper of paper as she leafed through the documents that had been contained in the file folder that now lay on the floor beside her.

She read slowly, carefully, scanning the words with intensity, until they began to dance before her eyes, and then she sat back, put her hands to her temples, and sighed deeply.

The papers proved what she'd known, all along. Edward Archer's threats had been just that—threats, nothing more. Olivia's Dream was hers, lock, stock and drapery rods. So long as she made her loan payments and mortgage payments on time, she had nothing to fear from anybody.

Why had she let him intimidate her so? She wasn't the sort of woman who could be driven into a corner— you couldn't be, not if you were going to get ahead in business. As for the rest . . .

Olivia got to her feet. She didn't even want to think about the rest, about how she'd let him force a response from her when he'd kissed her, so that she'd behaved exactly like the woman of low morals he'd accused her of being. All she could do was hope that he, even in his incredible arrogance, understood that she'd acted that way because she'd been distraught and confused, that her momentary weakness in his arms hadn't had a damned thing to do with him.

Not that it mattered. She would never have to face him again. He'd made threats, and that was it. He'd

known, all along, that he didn't have a leg to stand on.
The money Charles had lent to her was hers, so long as
she kept up her end of the repayment agreement, and
nobody, not even Archer, could do a thing about it.

As for the ugly things he believed about her relationship with his stepfather—well, that didn't surprise her.
The Edward Archers of this world were only too ready
to believe the worst. They were men of privilege and
money who thought girls—and women—of a different
class were toys that could be bought for a price.

Once he found out that it was Ria who'd been involved with his stepfather and not she, there would be
the satisfaction of rubbing his patrician nose in the
information.

Olivia sighed as she tucked the legal papers into their
folder. Well, that would have to wait for later. She
couldn't say anything about Ria, not until she'd talked
with her—and Ria wasn't talking to anybody just yet.
The only communication she'd had from her was a short
note delivered by messenger the day after Edward
Archer's explosive visit.

'Oh, Livvie, it's awful!' the note had said in Ria's
spidery hand. 'We'll talk soon, but right now I need to
be alone. I know you'll understand. Bless you.'

There was nothing to do but dig in and wait for Ria
to surface, Olivia thought as she put the folder in the
wall safe and closed the door. Until that happened, she'd
keep a stiff upper lip and go on about her business, which
was making Olivia's Dream succeed. And Edward Archer
could just take all his angry threats and——

'Olivia?'

Olivia clapped her hand to her heart and swung
around. Dulcie was standing in the open doorway, her
shoulder-bag on her arm, a steaming mug in her outstretched hand.

'Dulcie!' She gave a nervous laugh. 'You scared me
half to death. I thought you'd left an eternity ago.'

'Coffee? You look as if you could use some.'

'Thanks.' Olivia took the mug, blew lightly on the black liquid, then took a sip. 'Perfect. You're right, this is exactly what I needed.' She took another mouthful, then put the mug on her desk. 'What are you doing here?'

Dulcie walked into the room and leaned back against the desk. 'There's no easy way to tell you this,' she said. 'But—there's something you should see in today's *Chatterbox*.'

'That rag?' Olivia made a face. 'What could possibly be of interest to us in——?'

'It's—it's about Charles.'

'About Charles? But...' Olivia went very still. Why was Dulcie looking at her that way? 'Maybe you'd better tell me what the article was about,' she said softly.

'I hate these tabloids,' the girl said with sudden ferocity. 'They're just—just so sleazy. I mean, hey, the guy was your partner, that's all, he——'

'My backer. Charles Wright was my backer. He loaned me the start-up money to open this shop.' Olivia fought against the faint notes of panic in her voice. 'You know that.'

Her assistant's shoulders lifted and fell in an eloquent shrug. 'Sure. That's what I meant. And if he was anything else——'

'Dammit, Dulcie, what are you saying?'

'Listen, whose business is it if he—if you and he...?' Dulcie's face turned pink. 'I would never say anything, Olivia, not even if that guy from the *Chatterbox* came sniffing around. I'd just tell him I think he's a slimeball to have printed that stuff about you.'

Olivia felt the blood drain from her face. She reached out and grasped the back of the chair for support.

'About—about me?'

'Yeah.' Dulcie nodded unhappily. 'About—about you and Wright.'

'What kind of stuff?' Olivia touched the tip of her tongue to her lips. 'That he lent me the money to buy this place? Is that what you mean?'

Dulcie shook her head as she dug into her holdall and pulled out a folded newspaper.

'Here,' she mumbled. 'It's probably best if you read it yourself.'

Wordlessly, Olivia took the paper and looked at it. The bold print leaped at her accusingly.

'MILLIONAIRE FINANCIER FEATHERED A SECRET LOVE NEST', it said, and below, in slightly smaller letters, 'Sutton Place Home to Charles Wright and Dark-haired Mystery Woman'.

The paper shook in Olivia's hands as her eyes travelled down the page to a grainy black and white photo of a tall, slender woman, her back to the camera, her shoulder-length dark hair flying as she stepped from a low-slung sports car. 'Do You Know this Gorgeous Bird?' the caption asked.

Olivia caught her breath. Yes, she thought, I know her. Of course I know her.

It was Ria.

'You don't have to worry.'

Olivia blinked and looked up. Dulcie was watching her closely. 'Worry about what?' she said slowly.

Dulcie lifted her chin. 'I wouldn't tell a soul, not a single soul.'

'Good,' Olivia said absently, as she stared at the photo again. 'I wouldn't want anyone to know. It would be upsetting, with all the publicity and——'

'Oh, I understand.' Dulcie put her hand on Olivia's arm. 'Mr Wright would never have wanted to drag your name through the mud. Why, he always treated you so— so politely. No one would've guessed that you and he were—that you were...'

Olivia looked up in horror as the girl's voice faded. 'But this isn't me,' she said quickly. 'It's...'

It's Ria, she almost blurted. But Dulcie and Ria had never met—Ria had not been by since the shop had opened.

Besides, how could she say that without telling Dulcie everything?

She looked down at the photo again. Yes, it was Ria. But if you didn't know any better, you might easily have thought it was Olivia. Olivia, with her dark hair flying. Olivia, getting out of Charles Wright's little black Mercedes...

'It's not me,' she said again.

'Of course it isn't,' Dulcie said compassionately, but what she was really saying, what Olivia could clearly hear her saying, was, We both know it's you, Olivia, but if you don't want to admit it, I understand.

'I'd never judge you, and neither would anybody else with half a brain. If it were you they were talking about.' Dulcie touched her tongue to her lips. 'Which, of course, it isn't.'

Olivia looked up.

'This is the 1990s, not the Dark Ages.'

'That's—that's good to know. I—I...' Olivia swallowed drily. 'It's late,' she said softly. 'Why don't you head home? It was—it was kind of you to stay after hours.'

'Listen, if you need to talk... If you need a shoulder to lean on... Even tonight. I could stay a while, or we could go out for a bite...?'

'No,' Olivia said quickly, 'no, that's all right. You—you go on. I'm fine.'

'Sure?'

Olivia nodded. 'Sure,' she said. Somehow she managed to smile. 'I'm going to go upstairs, get into my robe, and make myself an omelette. Then I'll take a long, hot bath and climb into bed with a good book.'

It was a good prescription. But it was impossible to fill. Instead, she stood immobile in the centre of the room, listening to the tap of Dulcie's heels on the stairs, then to the muffled thud of the front door as it slammed shut, and then she sank down into the chair at her desk.

Dear heaven, what a mess! First Edward Archer, now Dulcie. Dulcie, of all people. How could she think such a thing? Never mind. She could survive it, at least until Ria surfaced and she could tell Dulcie the truth.

Olivia spread the newspaper on the desk. It was this that worried her, this article filled with sly innuendo and the photo that accompanied it. Papers like the *Chatterbox* prided themselves on the dogged determination with which they pursued stories, the sleazier the better. What if a reporter turned up at her door? What if——?

The sharp peal of the night buzzer broke her concentration. Olivia looked up, her heart pounding. A reporter? No. It couldn't be. There was no way anyone could put two and two together and come up with her name. Not so quickly, anyway.

Dulcie, she thought, as she made her way down the stairs. It would be just like her to have come back despite all Olivia's assurances that she'd be fine. All right, she thought as she opened the door, she'd ask the girl in for a cup of tea or a glass of wine, then send her off again.

'How can I turn you down?' she said as she opened the door. 'You're very sweet, and very persist——'

The words caught in her throat. It wasn't Dulcie standing in the faint glow of the street light. It was Edward Archer.

Olivia slammed both hands against the door and began shoving it closed. But he was quicker, and far stronger. He wedged one powerful shoulder between the door and the jamb and shoved back.

'Open the door, Miss Harris.'

'Get out of here!' Olivia gritted her teeth and jammed her hip against the wall. Her feet began sliding out from under her as she leaned all her weight against the door.

'Do—you—hear—me?' she panted. 'Go away, or I'll—I'll...'

'You'll what? Call the police?' He made a sound that might have been a laugh. 'We both know you won't do that.' He shifted his body and she felt the door giving way. 'Now, open the door before I break it down.'

He would do it, she thought bitterly. He was strong enough. And determined enough. He was the sort of man who would stop at nothing to get his own way.

He stepped into the darkened shop as soon as she stepped back. The door swung after him. Olivia started to reach past him to the light switch, but he grabbed her wrist.

'Who were you expecting?' he asked in a cold, soft voice.

Olivia's heart constricted. 'Let go of me.'

'A man,' he said flatly, answering his own question. His hand tightened and he stepped closer to her. She could smell the night and the darkness mixed with his own masculine scent. 'Another lover, Olivia, but I suppose you've waited long enough to get over your tragic loss.'

What was he trying to do? Frighten her? Did he want her to try and twist free of him, so that he could establish once again what they both already knew, that he could dominate her without any effort?

Well, she'd be damned if she'd give him the satisfaction.

'I said, let me go.' Her voice was low and steady, although her heart was thudding. After what seemed like an eternity, his hand fell away from her. She drew a shuddering breath as she switched on the light and stared at his cold, set face. 'All right,' she said, 'what do you want?'

His lips drew back from his teeth. 'Such poor manners, darling. Don't I get offered a drink? At the very least, you might offer me a chair. I've had a long day.'

He was standing too close to her. She didn't like having
to tip her head up, even just this little bit, to look him
in the face. And she didn't like the way they were
standing, either, she with her back to the wall, he with
that little curl of a smile on his mouth, the smile that
said—that said...

She walked by him to the area of the showroom where
clients could sit and discuss fabrics and décor, ignoring
a pair of handsome wing chairs drawn up cosily to a
round glass table, heading instead for a delicate pair of
grey suede loveseats that faced each other across a low
black marble table. It was an area she had designed especially for the pleasure of female clients. But it would
bring no comfort to Edward Archer. The loveseats were
too soft and low; he would sink down into the cushiony
depths and then have a choice between arranging his long
legs so that he either sat with his knees tucked under his
chin or stretched out at an awkward angle beneath the
table.

Either way, he'd be at a disadvantage. And she pre-
ferred it that way. So far, each time they'd confronted
each other, he'd held the winning hand because she'd
been playing *his* game, with *his* rules, a game that would
be impossible to win until she'd spoken to Ria. But she
could at least even the odds. She could be cool, self-
contained. She could use whatever was at hand to make
him look foolish. This very feminine setting, for instance. The thought made it easy to smile politely as she
turned and faced him.

'I take it you're not here to enquire about having us
design a room for you, Mr Archer?'

His teeth glinted as he laughed. 'No. Not quite.'

Olivia sat down on one of the loveseats, crossed her
ankles primly and folded her hands in her lap.

'Then why are you here?'

He didn't even give the little sofa opposite hers a
glance. Instead, he went behind it, put his hands flat on
the curved back, and leaned towards her. It was a causal
gesture that made him look at ease. It also emphasised

the broad line of his shoulders. And, she realised with a little click of irritation, it put her right back in the same place she'd been when they'd been standing near the door. She was, once again, forced to tilt back her head in order to look at him.

'I expected your fingers to be all stained with ink.'

Olivia's brow furrowed. 'What?'

A sly smiled curved across his mouth. 'Don't tell me no one's asked you to autograph today's *Chatterbox*, darling. I'd have thought you'd have writer's cramp by now.'

He'd seen the damned article, then. Her pulse quickened, but her answer was cool. She would not be intimidated this time.

'Can you really imagine me doing anything so tacky?'

He laughed softly. 'Actually, I can't. Come to think of it, I can't imagine you signing your name to anything but the back of a cheque.'

'Is that what you came to discuss? My handwriting?'

He stood up and walked slowly towards the cork-board that covered the full length of the rear wall.

'Your designs?' he asked, eyeing the room sketches and photos tacked on it.

'Mr Archer——'

'Nice.' He stroked his hand lightly over a couple of the sketches. 'Very nice, in fact.' He turned towards her. 'You do have a talent, then.' He chuckled softly. 'In addition to your more obvious one, I mean.'

Olivia rose to her feet. 'I asked you a question, Mr Archer. Why have you come here?'

'Edward.' He smiled as he walked towards her. 'Don't you think we should be on a first-name basis? Hell, we're almost related.'

'We are nothing to each other,' she said coldly.

'Aren't we?' He stopped in front of her. His smile tilted just a little. 'Surely, in this age of extended families, there's got to be a term that describes the relationship between a man and his stepfather's mistress.'

All her intentions to be cool and collected fled. 'I want you out of my home,' she said in a low voice. 'Do you hear me? I want you——'

'But it's not your home.'

'My shop, then. Don't play games with me, Mr Archer. You know what I mean.'

'Is that what you think this is, Olivia? A game?' He stepped forward quickly and caught hold of her arm. 'Yes,' he said softly, 'I suppose you do. That's how you've made your way in the world, isn't it? By playing "games" with men.'

'And is this the kind of game you play?' she asked, looking deliberately at where his fingers bit into her arm. 'Do you get your kicks out of mauling women?'

'I'm not mauling you, Olivia, I'm simply making sure I have your attention when I tell you what I want.'

'You're the one responsible for that—that ugly little piece in the paper, aren't you?' she demanded. Her jaw shot forward. 'You're the one who——'

'Don't be ridiculous,' he snapped. 'The last thing I want is to have Wright's name dragged through the mud.'

'Oh, sure.' Olivia's voice dripped sarcasm. 'I almost forgot. All that filial devotion.'

'You're being a fool! My mother bears the man's name—or had you forgotten all about old Charlie's little encumbrance?'

Olivia caught her breath as his hand tightened on her wrist. 'I told you,' she said through her teeth, 'he said he was getting a divorce.'

'Yes. Of course.' Edward laughed unpleasantly. 'Otherwise, you'd never have gotten involved with him. You're not the sort of girl to sleep with a married man.'

'Exactly,' she said, her face flushing with anger. 'I'm not.'

Edward grinned. 'Ah, but think of the rewards,' he said softly as he drew her closer. 'The thrill of meeting in secret, the little lies that add spice to each encounter...'

'Damn you!' Her breathing quickened as she struggled uselessly against him.

'Hell, you'd need something to compensate for—how shall I put it? For the law of diminished returns. A man Charlie's age, after all—how much excitement could he have brought to your bed, Olivia?'

'You son of a bitch,' she whispered.

'How do you keep yourself from growing bored, I wonder? Do you close your eyes and imagine yourself with a younger, more virile man?'

Olivia raised her flushed face to his. 'Are we back to that? I told you, I'd never in a million years imagine myself with you.'

He laughed as he slipped his arms around her and drew her against him. It was a game, at least it was at the beginning. But then her body brushed his, and she knew she'd made a mistake in baiting him. She felt the heat the instant he did; his eyes went dark and she felt him grow hard and aroused against her.

'No,' she whimpered, but it was too late. Edward was bending her back over his arm, catching her mouth with his, kissing her and kissing her until she caught fire and was consumed.

Her mouth parted to the sweet stroke of his tongue and the taste of him filled her. She made a sound in the back of her throat and he groaned and fell back against the wall still holding her, his kiss deepening, growing more fierce and impassioned as she leaned into him. His hand lifted, cupped her breast, and she moaned as she felt his fingers rub against her nipple.

She was trembling when he finally drew back. They looked at each other while the minutes sped by as rapidly as heartbeats, and then Edward drew a ragged breath.

'Damn you,' he said thickly. His hand slipped to her throat, then to her face. His fingers stroked lightly across her mouth, blazing a trail of fire on her flesh. 'Why should I want what other men have bought?'

Caught in a spasm of confusion and self-loathing, Olivia sought refuge in the avaricious identity he had given her.

'Perhaps because you know you can never afford it,' she said in a voice that seemed far too biting to be her own.

His hands tightened on her for a moment. He was in control again, she could see that in the coolness of both his smile and his eyes.

'Don't ever offer a challenge, Olivia,' he said softly. 'You might just find I'll take you up on it.'

When he let go of her, she stepped back quickly until half the length of the room separated them, and then she forced herself to meet his gaze.

'Why did you come here tonight?'

He waited a long while before he answered. 'I spoke to Wright's attorney today.'

Olivia crossed her arms over her breasts. 'Is that supposed to be of interest to me?'

He smiled tightly. 'We discussed Charlie's will.' He began pacing the room again, going from sketch to sketch, but it was easy to see that he wasn't really looking at any of them. 'I suppose you know what's in it, don't you? Women like you don't leave anything to chance. They spell out the price of a relationship before they enter into it.'

She drew herself up. 'Get to the point, please.'

'He left a little something to a couple of his "special friends".'

There was no mistaking the meaning of those words. Olivia glared at the man standing before her with that insolent smile on his lips.

'I wasn't one of his "special friends",' she said coldly. 'This doesn't concern me.'

'Of course it does, darling. The old boy forgave you your loan.'

The news stunned her. 'He what?'

Edward's mouth twisted. 'It was a generous gesture, wasn't it? Not as generous as his other gift, but——'

Olivia shook her head. 'I can't—I can't believe it! I never dreamed . . .'

'Aren't you tired of playing this game yet?' He moved closer to her. 'Charlie always treated his mistresses well.'

She stared at him. 'But I wasn't his mistress.'

'No?' He laughed unpleasantly. 'Who was, then? Your double?'

Ria, she thought desperately, it was Ria, not me . . .

His lip curled with disdain. 'What's the matter, darling? Cat got your tongue?'

'We were—we were just friends,' she said helplessly. 'Not even that. Acquaintances. Your stepfather and I——'

'You'll get formal notification, of course. From Wright's attorney.' His eyes swept over her, leaving her feeling soiled and naked. 'I just wanted the pleasure of breaking the news to you myself.'

'Mr Archer, if you'd just listen——'

'What could you possibly say that I'd be interested in hearing?' he said in a chill voice.

That I wasn't anything to your stepfather, Olivia thought.

'Mr Archer,' she began, then paused. He was watching her through narrowed eyes, disbelief and contempt etched into every hard angle of his face, and she knew that he'd never believe anything she said. His kind never did.

Besides, what did it matter what he thought? He was nothing but a vivid reminder of a childhood spent at the edge of his world.

She'd be damned if she gave him any explanation at all.

'You're quite right,' she said, her tone as frigid as his. 'I've nothing to say to you. Nothing at all.'

Something glinted, then went out, in his eyes. 'No.' Edward's voice went flat. 'I didn't think you would.'

She drew herself up. 'Goodbye, Mr Archer.'

'Old Charlie's tastes must have changed the past few months,' he said softly. She flinched as he reached out to her, but he only drew his hand lightly across her cheek. 'You're different from the women he usually took up with, I'll give you that much. That air of cool disdain, the "don't touch me" look, even the way you respond when a man kisses you, as if you've waited all your life for him and him alone...' He drew a ragged breath. 'If I ever had to pay for my women, I might be tempted to pick up where Wright left off.'

'There's not enough money in the world for you to buy me,' she said in a voice that trembled with barely suppressed fury.

He laughed. Laughed, damn him! And then, very slowly and deliberately, he bent down, twined his fingers into her hair, and kissed her.

'Goodnight, Olivia,' he said softly.

She stayed perfectly still as he walked past her to the door, listening as it opened, then closed. Then, very slowly and carefully, as if she were made of glass, Olivia walked to the door and double-locked it, and then she made her way up the stairs to her flat.

Once there, she stood in the darkness, stripped off her clothes and stepped into the shower, turning it as hot as she could, standing beneath the spray for a long, long time, until finally she felt cleansed, not just of Edward Archer's accusations but of his touch and the shameful way she had responded to it.

CHAPTER FOUR

DULCIE came in the next morning with a box of chocolate fudge from the gourmet shop up the street and an earnest apology.

'I'm sorry for what I said last night,' she said immediately, her face set in a series of down-turned lines. 'I was so busy telling you that whatever you did was your own business that I overlooked the most important thing.'

'You don't owe me an apology.'

Dulcie held up her hand. 'I was climbing into bed when I finally realised what you'd said—that the girl in that awful picture, the girl who was having an affair with Charles Wright, wasn't you.'

Olivia sighed. 'No. It wasn't,' she said in a low voice. 'It wasn't me at all. Apologies aren't necessary.' She put her hand on Dulcie's. 'I know you're my friend, and——'

'I'm just sorry I made that silly speech last night.'

'It wasn't silly,' Olivia said with a little smile. 'It was kind and generous, and I thank you for it.'

Dulcie grinned. 'Thank me for the fudge instead.' She put the box on Olivia's desk. 'It took real will-power and dedication not to eat all of it while I was bringing it here.'

Olivia laughed. 'You really are a true friend, Dulcie.'

The words were light. But as the week wore on, that friendship became Olivia's lifeline.

It was Dulcie who steadied her when the *Chatterbox* came out the next day. The first brief mention of Charles Wright's 'Mystery Woman' had only been the beginning, it seemed. The next item was longer and juicier; it dealt in loving detail with 'The Sutton Place Love

Nest,' and included tantalising hints about the mystery woman as glimpsed by a supermarket delivery boy who was sure he'd seen her once in the hallway.

'A really reliable eye-witness account,' Dulcie said lightly of the boy's description.

The mystery woman was young and very beautiful, he said. But so was a significant percentage of the female population in Manhattan.

And she was slender.

'Well, that really nails it home,' Dulcie said through her teeth.

Olivia made a valiant effort at waving it all away. She and Ria didn't actually look alike. The long, dark hair and slender figures were their only similarities. But rags like the *Chatterbox* mixed fact, fiction, and innuendo to serve their own needs. Reality—and the truth—apparently counted for very little.

'They spent a weekend here, in a little cottage by the shore,' the manager of an exclusive Fire Island resort said.

That item was about Ria, of course. She had once mentioned that she and Charles were going to the beach for the weekend.

'They had intimate lunches here all the time,' the head waiter at a restaurant in Greenwich Village confided.

That had been Olivia. But there'd only been two lunches, both about business, held in a place convenient to the architect's office.

'They always asked for the last booth,' the man gushed, 'and we knew better than to disturb them once we'd served their meal.'

Olivia barked out a word she'd never before used, ripped the page from the paper, and shredded it into a dozen pieces.

'It's a lie,' she said. 'A complete lie!'

And the lies kept coming, until even someone as new to the world of cheap gossip as Olivia sensed that the

Chatterbox was getting ready to slip over the thin line
that separated allegation from accusation.

She kept telling herself that Ria was going to come
popping out of the woodwork any moment and clarify
things. And she waited for the tireless *Chatterbox* reporter to realise that he was tracking down a story about
two different women. But either happening would have
been a miracle, and it was not a time for miracles.

And then, one morning, Dulcie came into the shop
and handed Olivia that day's paper.

'You'd better sit down,' she said softly.

'Is it very bad?' Olivia asked.

The girl nodded. 'On page three.'

Olivia took a deep breath, blew it out, then opened
the paper. She'd been anticipating this moment for days,
trying to prepare herself for whatever the worst might
be, but when she saw the quarter-page photo of herself
standing outside Olivia's Dream she turned white as a
sheet.

'Olivia Harris,' the bold print read, 'The Mystery
Woman in Married Financier's Life.' The rest of the
caption explained, in smaller print, that the head waiter
in the Village restaurant had been only too eager to
identify Olivia as the 'Mystery Woman'.

Olivia didn't know whether to laugh or cry. He'd only
been able to name her because she'd signed the charge
slips for some of those meals.

'They're business deductions,' she'd insisted when
Charles had reached for the bill—and now, her name
had come leaping off those receipts to hang her.

She sat staring at the photo for a long, long moment.
When she looked up at Dulcie, her eyes were very dark
against the paleness of her skin.

'I'll sue,' she said in a shaky whisper. 'I'll take those
sleazy bastards for every penny they have.'

'Take it easy, Olivia. Maybe—maybe this whole thing
will pass over without——'

The shrill of the telephone caught Dulcie in mid-sentence. It was a reporter for the *Enquirer* wanting an interview. By mid-morning, Olivia had taken the phone off the hook. What was the point in answering its persistent ring when she knew the caller would either be a reporter insisting on an interview or a client telling her in frigid tones that she had no intention of dealing with what one woman quaintly called 'a home-wrecker'?

That was the final straw.

'It's one thing to hope this blows over,' Olivia said furiously to Dulcie. 'It's another to sit back and let the shop go down the tubes.' She snatched up her bag and stalked to the door. 'I'm going to see my attorney and nail those bastards to the wall.'

Her attorney was sympathetic. But he had to tell her that there were no grounds for a lawsuit.

'Outfits like this are usually clever about dancing within the boundaries of the law, Miss Harris.' He jabbed a finger at the offending photo and the article that accompanied it. 'They never come out and call you Wright's lover, you see, they just say that he backed your shop with an undisclosed sum of money, that you and he were seen together often——'

'They say we had a "relationship",' she said, her eyes flashing with anger. 'Surely that's grounds for legal action.'

Her attorney shook his head. 'But you *did* have a relationship.'

'A business relationship! But the way they make it sound—— '

'That's how the game is played, I'm afraid. They say something perfectly acceptable while making it sound like something quite different.' He shrugged his shoulders. 'I really am sorry, Miss Harris, but there's nothing to be done unless they slip up and say something we can prove is libellous.'

Angry tears shone in Olivia's eyes. 'Like what?' she demanded, her voice breaking. 'Like—like a claim that I—I dance naked in the park?'

The man smiled sadly. 'Actually, I had a case like that once. It looked pretty good, too—until my client mentioned that of course she hadn't done anything like that since she was three years old. Well, that changed things. After all, she *had* danced naked in the park, and——'

For the second time that day, Olivia used a word that made even the lawyer blush.

'Never mind,' she snapped. 'I'll find a way to deal with this myself.'

But it was an empty threat. What could she do? she thought as she paced from one end of her tiny flat to the other that evening. Ria held the key to everything, and where was she?

Damn Ria anyway! Olivia came to a halt in the centre of her tiny living-room. She had to know what was going on; why hadn't she come forward?

Maybe it was time to stop worrying about Ria and start worrying about herself. Yes. Maybe it was. Maybe...

She groaned and closed her eyes. Even if she were willing to tell the real story to the world, what good would it do? Things had gone too far. Without Ria around to corroborate her story, it would only look as if she were trying to lie herself out of a bad situation.

The phone clamoured as it had been doing all evening. Tomorrow, Olivia thought grimly as she strode towards the bedroom to answer it, tomorrow she'd call the phone company and get an unlisted number.

She snatched up the receiver and glowered at it.

'Whoever this is,' she said coldly, 'I am not interested in an interview. Or a photo shoot. Or posing for Playgirl of the——'

'Livvie?'

Olivia sank down on the edge of her bed. 'Ria! Where are you?'

'At Kennedy Airport. Look, Livvie, I'm sorry for this mess. But I'm not ready to——'

'Ria, listen to me. You've got to come back. Everything is falling apart here. I'm taking all the blame for you.'

'No. I can't. Not yet. Mommy and Daddy would go crazy.'

Olivia jumped to her feet. 'Mommy and Daddy? What about me? Have you seen the paper today?'

'They think I'm on vacation, Livvie. Don't spoil things, please.'

'Ria. Ria, dammit——'

'I'll pay you back, I swear,' Ria whispered, and the phone went dead.

'Ria? Ria!'

Silence. Olivia made a sound that was as much a sob as it was a cry of anger and slammed down the receiver. It rang almost immediately, and she snatched it up again.

'Listen here, Ria——'

'It's not Ria, darling.'

The voice was unmistakable. It belonged to Edward Archer. Olivia stared at the telephone as if it had suddenly grown claws and a tail, and then she drew a deep breath.

'I've nothing to say to you, Mr Archer,' she said coldly. 'I thought I made that quite clear.'

'And I thought we were on a first-name basis.' He laughed softly and she could almost see him in front of her, that hard, handsome face with the teasing smile tilting at his mouth.

She sank down on the bed again, one hand cradling the phone and the other at her forehead.

'What do you want?' she asked wearily.

There was a second's pause. When he spoke again, there was just a hint of softness in his voice.

'You sound tired, Olivia.'

'Yes. Well, it's been a long day.'

'The article in that damned paper, you mean? Yes, I saw it.'

'Did you?' She gave a sharp laugh. 'Actually, I thought you might have written it.'

'Olivia. I need to see you.'

She laughed again. 'Goodnight, Edward.'

'Don't hang up,' he said sharply. 'Didn't you hear what I said? I have to see you. Tonight. Do you know Noah's Ark on Sixty-Third and First?'

'I have no intention of meeting you.' Her voice took on a chill. 'Why are you bothering to call? When you wanted to see me before, you—you forced your way into my house, like—like——'

'I thought it would be best if we met on neutral ground.' A sexy huskiness seeped into his voice. 'Just so we don't get sidetracked.'

Colour leaped into her cheeks. 'I don't know what you mean,' she said stiffly.

She heard the soft hiss of his breath. 'Don't you?'

The memory of his kiss swept through her. She closed her eyes and took a deep breath.

'I've nothing to say to you. Please don't call me any more.'

'Wait, Olivia. Don't hang up.'

'Give me one good reason not to.'

'I know about Ria Bascomb,' he said.

Olivia touched the tip of her tongue to her lips. 'I'll meet you,' she whispered.

He laughed with obvious satisfaction. 'I knew you would, darling,' he said, and the phone went dead.

Noah's Ark was a popular and trendy East Side watering hole, and even though she'd never been there Olivia could have described it within an inch of accuracy.

It was small and smoky, with loud, fast music blaring from an expensive sound system behind the bar. And it was packed, even on a weekday night, with good-looking men and attractive women, all smiling winning smiles, determined to impress the life out of each other. She saw Edward right away, despite the smoke and the jam of bodies. He was leaning against the bar with a glass of something dark in his hand, half a head taller than the men around him—and twice as handsome.

Olivia's breath caught. Why had she thought that? A wave of colour beat into her cheeks and just at that moment, as if he'd heard her thoughts, Edward's gaze lifted to the mirror and met hers. Olivia felt the breath rush from her lungs. The world seemed to stand still while they looked at each other, and then he smiled, lifted his glass in salute, and drained its contents.

She felt her heart leap within her breast as he put the glass down and stepped away from the bar. A woman sitting near him looked up, saw him in the mirror, and gave him a quick, intimate smile, but Edward never noticed it. His eyes were riveted on Olivia.

A *frisson* of pleasure whispered along her skin. It didn't make any sense, that she should feel this way. Even though he knew the truth now, that it had been Ria and not she who'd been his stepfather's mistress, Edward had said things, done things, that could not be forgiven.

But still. Oh, but still. He was so handsome. And exciting. Every woman here knew it, she could see it in the way they watched him. Her hand went to her hair. She'd left it loose and it hung around her face like a soft, dark cloud. And, as he drew nearer, she was suddenly glad she hadn't put on the jeans and sweatshirt that had been her first instinct, but had taken the extra time to slip into a pair of slender black heels and a wine-red silk dress with a black wool coat worn open over it.

Edward was taking it all in as he approached her, she could see it in his face. A little smile, the one she remembered, curled across his mouth and again a little tremor danced along her spine.

His smile tilted crookedly when he reached her side.

'I'm glad you came,' he said softly. 'I'm sorry to have called so late, but——'

'That's—that's all right.'

His fingers were cool against the nape of her neck as he drew the coat from her shoulders.

'You look very beautiful, Olivia.'

Her throat constricted. 'Thank you. I—I had to change. That's why I'm a little late——'

'Ah.' He smiled into her eyes. 'You were already in bed when I phoned, then.'

She looked up quickly, searching his face for some hidden meaning. When she found none, she smiled back at him.

'No. No, I wasn't. But I wasn't dressed for——'

'Dressed or undressed, you would be the most beautiful woman I've ever seen.'

She felt the swift rush of colour rise under her skin. His words had been provocative, yet somehow not offensive, and a little voice whispered a warning. Be careful, oh, be careful, it said. Nothing's changed, not yet. He thought you were a slut the moment he met you, remember?

But her skin was on fire where his fingers touched it.

He led her to a dark little corner in the rear of the café, his hand firm on her elbow, his body very close to hers as they made their way through the densely packed crowd, and as he helped her into a chair, his hand lingered on her arm.

'What would you like to drink?'

Olivia hesitated. 'I don't know. White wine, I suppose.'

'The lady will have a glass of Chardonnay,' he said to the waitress. 'And I'll have another double whiskey.' He leaned across the table. 'I wasn't sure you'd come,' he said.

She looked at him. 'You knew I would, Edward.'

'Did I?'

'Yes. You said you knew about——'

'Of course.' His smile flattened. 'I said the magic words, that's why you agreed to meet me, isn't it?' He fell silent as their drinks were served, and then he lifted his glass and held it out. After a moment, she lifted hers. 'What shall we drink to, darling?' he said, and before she could answer, he winked. 'I know. To the magic words. To Ria Bascomb.'

Olivia took a sip of wine as he drank down half his whiskey. 'Edward,' she began, 'how did you——?'

'What's the matter? Isn't the wine to your liking?' He nodded wisely. 'Sorry, I should have remembered. You prefer champagne. You were drinking it the day we met.'

She smiled slightly. 'Yes. I remember.'

'I remember, too.' He took another mouthful of whiskey. 'Olivia, the Ice Queen.' He gave an exaggerated shudder. 'God, but you almost froze me to death when I asked you to have lunch with me.'

Her smile grew fixed. 'I told you, I had an appointment.'

'Yes, I know.' Was it her imagination, or was there a sudden edge to his voice? 'With my stepfather.'

'And with Ria,' she said, her eyes meeting his squarely. 'But then, you must know that now.'

'Yes,' he said softly, 'oh, yes, Olivia. I know all about it.'

Something was wrong. She had come expecting—expecting what? Not an apology, perhaps, nor even vindication, but——

'Aren't you going to drink your wine?'

She blinked at the sudden change in conversation. 'Yes. Yes, I will.' She lifted the glass and took a sip. Her hand was unsteady, and a little of the pale liquid sloshed on to her fingers. She started to wipe it off on her napkin, but Edward caught hold of her wrist.

'Don't waste it,' he said softly, bringing her hand to his lips.

Her breath caught as he drew her fingers, one at a time, into the heat of his mouth. Flame shot through her, arcing from her fingertips to her breasts and then down into her very core.

'Edward, please——'

'Please what?' he whispered, his fingers stroking the soft flesh at the base of her thumb. 'Please take me somewhere so we can be alone? Please strip off my pretty dress and touch me?' His eyes dropped to where her breasts thrust against the red silk and he smiled. 'Have you ever had a man lick drops of champagne from the hollow between your breasts, Olivia?' She tried to pull her hand free, but he wouldn't let her. 'The salt of your skin and the sweetness of the wine would be a heady mixture,' he said hoarsely, and all at once, with a little sense of despair, she realised that he was drunk, or awfully close to it.

She pulled against his grasp. This time he let her go, and she dropped her hand into her lap and clenched her fingers tightly, her nails pressing almost painfully into her palm.

'You—you were going to tell me how you found out about Ria and your stepfather.'

He grinned. 'And you, darling. Don't leave that out. I remember enough of my boyhood lessons to know that a triangle has three sides.'

Her eyes met his. 'What's that supposed to mean?'

'I thought you wanted to know how I found out about Ria,' he said as he signalled the waitress for a refill. One dark brow rose as he looked at her. 'It certainly wasn't from you, darling. You were as closed as a clam about your old friend.'

Olivia nodded. 'I—I couldn't say anything,' she said, leaning towards him. 'I mean, how could I do such a thing to her? We've known each other since we were children, and——'

'You wanted to protect her.' Edward paused as the waitress took up his empty glass and put a full one down in its place. 'Yes, I suppose that's admirable. You've no one to answer to. That's one of the advantages of being your kind of woman, isn't it?'

She stared across the table at him. His expression was unreadable, as dark and fathomless as his eyes. Olivia's heart seemed to constrict.

'After all, Miss Bascomb has a family and social position to live up to. You——' He shrugged again. 'You can do whatever you like.' He laughed softly. 'And we both know what it is you like, don't we, baby?'

Nothing had changed. Nothing at all. Hope, or whatever it was that had risen within her when she'd first seen him tonight, collapsed within her like a balloon under the prick of a pin. She started to shove back her chair, but Edward reached out and caught her wrist.

'Where is she?' he demanded.

'Who?'

'Your pal. Ria.'

'I've no idea. And if you don't let go of me——'

'Wright was very good to her, Olivia. Very, very good.'

'Dammit, Edward——'

'He left her stock in Gemini.'

She stared at him. 'Am I supposed to know what that means?'

'It's the company my father founded.' His expression grew grim. 'The one Wright had been milking for years. That stock—the company belongs to my mother.'

'Well—well, I'm sorry if that's so, but——'

'I want that stock, Olivia.' His fingers tightened on her wrist. 'And I'll get it. I'll see to it that your pal Ria signs over each certificate.'

Her eyes flashed fire. 'I'm sure you will. Now, let go of me!'

'I asked you a question, dammit. Where is she?'

'And I gave you an answer. I don't know where she is.' Her chin lifted. 'And if I did, I wouldn't tell you.'

Edward's teeth flashed in a mirthless grin. 'What a pair! She got the stock, you got your "loan" forgiven.'

'It *was* a loan, dammit!' Olivia twisted her hand free of his. 'If you don't believe me, check with my accountant. Or my bank. Or your stepfather's accountants. I've already made a payment, and I'll continue to make them, just as we agreed.'

He laughed. 'And in twenty years you'll have repaid it all. That's not a loan, it's a gift. A man doesn't give that kind of money to a woman with no business history and no collateral.' His gaze swept over her. 'Unless it was for extraordinary services rendered.'

She stared at him, as trapped for the moment by his dark, angry eyes as she would have been by the press of his hand on hers, and then, with an abrupt shove, Olivia pushed her chair back from the table.

'Goodnight, Mr Archer.' He caught her arm as she rose. 'Let go of me,' she spat.

Edward got to his feet. There was a dark crimson flush across his high cheeks.

'A question first,' he said, without preamble. 'Do you know anything about feelings? Real feelings?'

'What?'

'Tell me about emotions, Olivia. Tell me what you felt in Wright's arms.' His mouth twisted. 'Or in mine.'

Olivia flung back her head. 'Nothing,' she said through her teeth. 'Not one thing.'

'Damn you!' Edward's fingers tightened almost painfully on hers. 'It's all lies, isn't it? That little moan of surrender when you kiss me, the way your body melts against mine...'

'Hey, hey!' Olivia and Edward whirled around. A burly man, his arm tightly wrapped around the shoulder of a giggling redhead, was playfully wagging his finger at them. 'Can't block the aisle, kids. Gotta leave room for folks comin' through, you know.'

Edward glared at the intruders, then blew out his breath. 'Right,' he said grimly. He let go of Olivia's hand and stepped back. 'Sorry.'

Olivia snatched her coat from the chair and spun around. Edward's voice rose after her, but she kept going, out of the door and to the street. There was a taxi at the kerb and she flew inside and gave the driver her address.

'Hurry, please,' she said.

It took only minutes to reach her town house. She glanced over her shoulder after the cab sped away. The street was deserted. Edward hadn't followed her, then. With a sigh of relief, she fumbled her key from her purse.

Brakes squealed as a low-slung black car rounded the corner. Olivia caught her breath.

'Edward,' she whispered.

Heart pounding, she inserted the key into the lock. But it was too late. He was out of his car and beside her, swinging her around to face him with ungentle hands.

'Don't touch me,' she said in a low, dangerous voice. 'I promise you, I *will* call the police this time.'

Edward laughed. 'Go on, then. Do it. Yell for the cops at the top of your lungs.'

Olivia grimaced as she struggled against him. 'Don't push me, Edward, or I will! I'll tell them that—that I heard footsteps behind me,' she panted, 'that you—you followed me home——'

'And I'll tell them who you are. You're a genuine New York celebrity, Olivia, don't you realise that?' He drew her hands behind her and pushed her deep into the shadows of the doorway. 'I'll explain that you get a kick out of playing rough, that tonight things just got a little out of hand.'

'Damn you!' She stared up at him, her face white. 'What do you want from me, Edward?'

He looked at her in the silence of a long moment, his shoulders blocking the light from the street lamp.

'Maybe what you gave old Charlie,' he said finally, shifting his weight so his body was brushing against hers. 'But not on the same terms. When you come to my bed, it will be because you know I'm the only man who can make you feel what you've been faking for so long, not because you want what's in my bank account.'

'You don't know what you're talking about!'

'I know that you and Ria were both sleeping with my stepfather.'

'No!' Her anguished cry rose into the night. 'No, that's a lie. I never——'

'One at a time, of course.' He caught her face in his hand and tilted it up. 'After all, you're an old-fashioned girl, aren't you?'

'You filthy-minded bastard!'

'But it would have had to be that way. A woman like you would need a man's undivided attention.'

He bent towards her; she smelt the whiskey on his breath and then his mouth crushed hers. She twisted her head to one side, but there was no escaping his kiss.

God, how she hated this man! How she despised him! How she—how she...

A little shudder went through her, and then another. His mouth was moving on hers, the tip of his tongue stroking lightly, asking for access. His arms had gone around her; he was holding her close to him, so close that she could feel the heavy beat of his heart against her breast.

'Open to me,' he whispered against her mouth. 'Let me taste you, Olivia.'

No, she thought, no, no, no...

But her lips were parting under the silken demand of his, and with a little moan, she felt his tongue slide into her mouth.

He tasted of rage and of whiskey, of desire and of the night. He whispered her name again and again; his hand slid under her coat and she felt her breasts swell under his seeking touch, felt her body leap to blazing life as he caressed her. She was spinning out of control and had been for days, for weeks, from the instant he'd come storming into her life.

She hated him, not just for what he thought she was but for who *he* was, a man whose birthright gave him power and privilege, and who was sure he could use that power to do whatever he damned well pleased with her. She had grown up with his kind, she had learned early on what men like him thought of girls like her.

A sob rose in her throat. And here she was, proving him right. Here she was, in his arms, straining towards him.

Anger, not just at Edward but at herself, gave Olivia new strength. Her teeth clamped down on his lip.

'Ow!' He sprang back and put his hand to his mouth. 'What the hell...?'

'Stay away from me, Edward,' she said. 'Get out of my life and don't come back.'

He stared at her as he reached into his pocket and drew out a handkerchief. He touched it to his mouth. Olivia held her breath, waiting for his reaction. It came, after a moment, but it wasn't the anger she'd expected.

Instead, he looked at her and smiled crookedly. 'Did Charles like it when you played rough?'

'Did you hear me, Edward? I don't want to see you again.'

'All right.' Her voice surprised her. It was steady, calm, almost impersonal. 'I'll make a deal with you, Olivia. I want that stock back. It belongs to my family——'

'It isn't mine. You know that.'

'What I know is that it's your pal's, but I can't find her. She's out there playing hide and seek.'

'That's got nothing to do with me.'

Edward smiled again. 'But it has, darling. You know where she is.'

Olivia tossed her head. 'Maybe,' she said, more prideful than intelligent.

'Give her a message. Tell her I want her to sign the stock over to me. Tell her I want to see her immediately. Tell her——'

'Tell her yourself,' she said, tossing her head again, 'if you can find her,' and then she spun around, shoved open the door, and flew into the safety of the darkened house.

CHAPTER FIVE

OLIVIA'S mother had a saying, one that had soothed away the scraped-knee and cut-finger disasters of childhood.

'This will pass, sweetie,' she'd say, holding Olivia in her arms. 'Just think good thoughts, and before you know it the sun will shine again.'

At ten, when a car accident had taken Olivia's parents from her, remembering those softly murmured words had kept her going, especially after she'd been whisked off to the Bascomb house to become ward to a great-aunt she'd only seen a couple of times before.

This will pass, she'd told herself of the upheaval in her young life. And it *had* passed, after a while. The memory of her parents had been tucked away in her heart to carry with her always while she'd adapted to the reality of being raised by Great-Aunt Miriam, who'd been kind enough, if somewhat remote. And then Ria Bascomb had befriended her, and warmth had entered Olivia's life again.

Olivia had gone from childhood to womanhood; she'd studied hard and made a career and a life for herself. She had never once faltered, not even when her great-aunt had passed away, nor when it had become clear that Ria's life and her own had taken divergent paths. And she had never again needed to dredge up that old childhood litany.

Until now. She found herself thinking it the next day, when one glance at Dulcie's face told her there was another awful article in the *Chatterbox*.

'You don't have to look at it,' Dulcie said.

But she did. Not looking was the same as trying to keep your tongue from returning to an aching tooth.

The bold print was bad enough. There was her name, spelled out for the world to see. 'The Elusive Olivia Harris', it said, and she scanned only the first paragraph before hurling the paper against the studio wall.

'I'll hold down the fort here,' Dulcie said. 'You go upstairs.'

She did, returning to the design studio where she sat hunched over her drafting table, pretending to work while, each time the telephone rang, it was a notification to cancel an order. Olivia toyed with the idea of taking it off the hook, but what good was a business without a telephone?

You haven't got a business any more, a little demon said, you've got a three-ring circus.

By late afternoon, it seemed as if everybody in New York had called. But it wasn't true. Two people, at least, had *not* called. One was Ria.

The other was Edward Archer.

Why hadn't Ria phoned? Olivia ripped another useless sketch from her pad. Surely no one in the Western hemisphere could have missed what was happening here. Ria had to know what the *Chatterbox* and the TV tabloid shows were doing to her, she had to be aware that Olivia's head was on the chopping block.

But Ria was among the missing.

Edward was, too. That surprised her. He had asked her to give a message to Ria.

No. That wasn't quite accurate. He'd demanded she give a message to Ria, and she had refused. It was hard to imagine his leaving it at that. He was not a man to give up that easily.

She was certain he would contact her again. And this time, she thought with a sigh, she wouldn't be as pigheaded as she'd been last night. Instead of being stubborn, she'd tell him straight out that she had no idea how to get in touch with Ria.

The phone shrilled. 'Dammit,' she said through her teeth, and she snatched it up.

A man's voice crooned her name. 'Oh-liv-eee-aaah,' he said, and followed with a string of whispered suggestions that turned her face crimson.

She slammed down the receiver, shoved back her chair, and strode across the studio. Muttering under her breath, she threw on a hooded anorak, then trotted down the stairs.

'I'm going out,' she snapped as she made her way past Dulcie.

'Out? But——'

'And you might as well close up and go home.'

Her assistant stared after her. 'But this is our late night——'

Olivia wrenched open the door and stepped outside. She was halfway down the block when a mini-van from WGRZ-TV came barrelling down the street. Her heart tumbled. She forced herself not to run, to keep to a steady pace, but once she'd made it around the corner she began to move more quickly.

She had to go somewhere and think, but where? Where could she be faceless in this city? Central Park was not far, but it was almost sundown. That wasn't a time to be in a city park. She stepped blindly from the kerb. Think, she told herself, think...

A horn blared crazily. Olivia let out a yell and leapt back on to the pavement, out of the way of a sleek black automobile that came to a screeching stop.

'Hey!' Olivia was trembling. She didn't know if it was from the mess her life was fast becoming or from having almost been run over, but it didn't much matter. It felt good to raise her voice, damned good, and she jammed her hands on her hips and raised it again. 'Are you crazy? You almost...'

Her angry words faded. She knew this car, and she knew the driver. She turned to flee, but it was too late. Edward had already thrown open his door and scrambled from behind the wheel. His hands clasped her shoulders and he spun her towards him.

'Am *I* crazy?' he demanded, thrusting his white, furious face towards her. 'You came sleepwalking into traffic——'

'What do you think this is, a race-track? There's a light, in case you didn't——'

'Right. And red means stop—or is that too hard for you to understand?'

'Listen here, Mr Archer——'

'No. *You* listen, Miss Harris.' His fingers bit into her. 'The last thing I need right now is——'

'Don't you yell at me,' she said fiercely.

'I am not yelling,' he shouted. A horn shrilled behind his car, which was blocking traffic. Edward turned and gave the driver a furious look, and then he clasped Olivia's arm. 'Let's go.'

'I am not going anywhere with you,' she said, twisting in his grasp.

'Yes, you are,' he said grimly as he yanked open the passenger door. 'You're a danger to yourself and everybody else.'

'Dammit, I am not——'

Edward gritted his teeth. 'Get in the car,' he said, 'or so help me, I'll pick you up and put you in!'

She glared at him, but she could see that he meant every word. With a toss of her head, she wrenched free of his hand and flung herself inside. Edward slammed the door, then strode around to the driver's side and got behind the wheel. He stepped down hard on the gas and the car shot into traffic.

They drove in taut silence for a while before he spoke.

'What in hell did you think you were doing back there?'

'That's none of your business.'

'You made it my business, when you tried to become my hood ornament. Where were you going in such a damned fool rush?'

'To—to the park,' she said, staring straight ahead.

'The park? Central Park?' Edward laughed sharply. 'Are you nuts, or do you just like to live dangerously?'

She sighed and slipped down a little in the seat. His fingers drummed on the steering-wheel as they drew up to a light.

'That's all I'd have needed,' he said grimly, 'to run you down. God, I can see the headlines now. "Stepson Runs Down Stepfather's..."'

Olivia swivelled towards him. 'Stop it,' she hissed angrily.

Edward glanced at her. 'Yeah,' he said. He thrust his hand into his hair and blew out his breath. 'Look, it's been a rough day, and——'

'Tell me about it. My phone hasn't stopped ringing, there's a battalion of news hounds setting up camp outside my house——'

'You don't think you're the only one who's been facing a battery of lunatics, do you?'

She had, in fact, been thinking precisely that. Now, for the first time, it occurred to her that Edward, as Charles Wright's stepson, must be under the same pressure, too. And then, she thought suddenly, there was Edward's mother.

She put her hand to her forehead as the car began moving again. Ria, she thought, Ria, where are you? And why haven't you come forward?

'They're—they're like sharks when there's blood in the water,' she murmured. 'I never dreamed——'

'Olivia, we have to talk.'

'I know what you want, Edward.'

'Do you?' His laughter sounded strained. 'Somehow, I don't think so.'

'You want to know if I gave your message to Ria.' She took a deep breath. 'Well, I didn't.'

His laughter didn't sound as forced this time. 'I'm not really surprised. I get the feeling you're not a woman who takes kindly to being bossed around.'

That wasn't what he'd said last night. She closed her eyes. Last night he'd made it clear what he thought of her kind of woman; he'd——

'Have you had dinner yet?'

Her lashes lifted and she stared at him. Dinner? She hadn't even had breakfast, unless you counted the endless cups of coffee she'd been gulping all day.

'No,' she said. 'Not yet.'

'Neither have I.' He swung the wheel to the right. 'What do you want? Steaks? Seafood?'

Olivia's brows lifted. 'What's that supposed to mean?'

'It means that I have to eat and so do you, and we might as well do it together.' He glanced at her. 'Unless,' he said coldly, 'you've better plans for the evening.'

She stiffened. 'Certainly. I intended to dine with a couple of millionaires.' She swung around and glared out of the windscreen. 'I'd sooner starve than eat with you.'

A muscle worked in his jaw. 'All right. I'll eat, you watch.'

Olivia sighed. She was weary, unhappy, and, now that she thought about it, she was hungry, too.

'OK,' she said, 'but buying me a meal doesn't mean——'

'—anything,' he said. 'I know.'

A smile of satisfaction angled across his mouth. She settled back as he manoeuvred the car through rush-hour traffic, and lay her head back against the seat. What had he been doing in her neighbourhood? she wondered suddenly. Had he been on his way to see her? He had to be pretty desperate to have come seeking her when he despised her still, even though he knew it was Ria who'd been left his precious Gemini stock. But then, girls not born with silver spoons in their mouths were never given the benefit of the doubt.

She closed her eyes wearily. She'd learned that the hard way in her teen years. Ria had been away at boarding-school by then, and Olivia had been desperately lonely.

Her aunt had been remote as always, seemingly more involved with supervising the Bascomb household than with raising a young niece, and it had become painfully obvious that the girls she'd grown up with had been Ria's friends and not hers.

Then, almost overnight, her childish body had become a series of lush young curves and the phone in her aunt's quarters had begun to ring, with calls from boys she and Ria had grown up with, all of them eager to ask her out.

Olivia had been flattered and happy. She'd envisaged football dates, homecoming parties, proms and holiday balls. She and Ria would double-date together when Ria came home for the summer.

But invitations like those never materialised.

'How about a movie tonight, Livvie?' a boy would say.

It hadn't taken long to realise that what they *really* meant was, How about a little fun and games in the back of my car, Livvie?

When she'd made it clear she wasn't interested, they were shocked. Who did she think she was? Not one of them, certainly. She was a nobody. They *knew* what kind of girl she was.

And so did Edward Archer. Olivia opened her eyes and looked across at him. He had not hesitated for so much as a moment in his assessment of her, but then, why would he? His kind were always so damned sure of themselves, sure of the judgements they made of other people.

Nothing had changed over the years, at least not so far as the Edward Archers of the world were concerned. But *she* had changed. She had become someone, she had built a life and a reputation for herself, a reputation that was suddenly under the cruellest kind of attack...

'...day and night?'

Olivia blinked and looked up. 'Did you say something?'

'I said, our dedicated journalists ought to be horse-whipped for hounding their quarry day and night.'

She nodded. 'They're very determined.'

'Determined is a polite way of putting it,' he said grimly. 'You were right when you called them sharks. They feed on misfortune. I keep thinking it's a damned good thing I convinced my mother to spend a few weeks with her sister in Palm Beach.'

Olivia angled towards him. 'Yes,' she said softly, 'I was thinking earlier that it must be difficult for you.'

Edward shrugged his shoulders. 'I'm not the story they want. But they'd love to have five minutes alone with the Widow Wright.'

'But that's awful. She's still in mourning. She shouldn't have to deal with all this ugly gossip and——'

Olivia's words faded to silence at the look Edward gave her.

'Such a touching sentiment,' he said coldly. 'You almost sound as if you mean it.'

Colour crimsoned her cheeks. How could she have been so stupid? She'd been his stepfather's mistress, as far as he was concerned.

She turned and stared out of the window.

'Where is this restaurant anyway?' she asked in a voice gone as flat and cold as his.

'Right here.' He swung his car into an underground garage, then into a parking slot and shut off the engine. 'OK. Let's go.'

Olivia looked up as Edward opened the door. She frowned as she followed him towards a bank of lifts.

'Where are we going?'

His hand closed on her elbow. 'I told you. To have something to eat. And to talk.'

The lift door slid open. Edward manoeuvred her inside, then pressed the penthouse level button. Olivia swung towards him.

'What kind of restaurant is this?' she demanded.

'It isn't,' he said crisply, 'it's my apartment.'

She slammed her hand against the button, and the lift shuddered to a halt.

'What in hell are you doing?'

'I am going home,' she said frigidly. She punched the lobby indicator, then punched it again. 'Just as soon as this—this miserable contraption starts moving.'

'You're not going anywhere until we've talked.'

'Don't play me for a fool, Edward.' Her mouth twisted. 'Talk is something you do in public places.'

'So is being recognised by gossip mongers.' He caught her chin and forced her to look at him. 'My apartment's the only place I could think of where we can talk without wondering if the sharks are in the water.'

'That's crazy!'

He gave her a quick, cold smile. 'Is it?'

They rode the rest of the way in silence, while she imagined what she'd see when the lift stopped. That he lived on the penthouse level didn't surprise her. The apartment would be huge, perfectly furnished and appointed, with a full retinue of servants. Dinner, even a last-minute dinner, would be a five-course affair, with a different wine for each course.

Had he expected her to be impressed? If he had, he'd underestimated her...

The doors slid open. Olivia blinked. Someone had underestimated someone, but suddenly she was uncertain as to who it was.

The foyer, and the living-room beyond, were large, certainly, and might even be called elegant. But there was no pretension about the furnishings or decorating scheme. Her eyes swept across the room, taking in the contemporary leather sling chairs that flanked a handsome Adam table, the Ming vase that sat beside a Remington bronze.

The place had a lived-in, comfortable look, and a complexity that mirrored its owner. She knew immediately and instinctively that no one but Edward Archer had selected any of the things that made this place his home.

She'd been wrong about the servants, too. There was only a houseman who offered her a drink while Edward went off to change. Olivia declined, and the man vanished. Alone, she strolled slowly around the handsome room, admiring the view of the city visible from two walls of wrap-around glass and the prints on the wall. It was an eclectic collection. A Russell, a Degas...

A splash of vivid colour on the far wall caught her eye. It was a Chagall. She made her way across the room and stood before the canvas, then very lightly touched her fingers to the frame.

'Do you like Chagall?'

'Oh, yes,' she said, spinning towards the sound of Edward's voice, 'very much. And this is especially...'

She fell silent. Edward was standing in the doorway, watching her with a little smile on his face. He had traded his tailored business suit for faded jeans that fitted him like a second skin and a cotton shirt the colour of his eyes, the collar undone several buttons to reveal a strong, tanned throat, the sleeves rolled back above muscular forearms.

Olivia swallowed drily as she looked at him. He must have taken a quick shower, she thought; his hair was still damp and a dark lock of it drooped over his forehead. I could brush it back, she thought suddenly, I could walk across the room to him and let my fingers whisper across his hair, I could rise up on my toes and press my mouth to his skin, I could...

A tremor went through her and she turned quickly away.

'We're not here to discuss art,' she said in a voice so cold it sounded unlike her own.

There was silence for a long moment, and then she heard the rasp of Edward's breath.

'No,' he said, just as coldly, 'we're not,' and he brushed past her towards the dining-room.

* * *

She had no intention of eating, even though dinner was not a five-course affair. It was, rather, steaks, baked potatoes, and salad. And there was only one bottle of wine, a red that gleamed like rubies when Edward poured it into two crystal wine glasses.

Olivia's mouth filled with saliva. No, she told herself sternly, and she folded her hands in her lap.

Edward watched her across the candle-lit table. 'Is there a problem with your steak?' he asked politely.

'I told you, I'm not hungry.'

'If you'd prefer something else——'

'No. No, thank you.'

'Carl can whip up an omelette, if you like.'

'This is fine,' she said tightly.

His brows rose. 'Then why aren't you eating?'

Olivia rolled her eyes to the ceiling, picked up her knife and fork, and cut into her steak. She stabbed the first bite into her mouth and chewed it angrily. It was good. Well, perhaps she'd eat a little. Just a bit.

She ate it all, and when she was done, she looked up.

'I guess I was hungrier than I realised,' she said defensively, but her breath caught when she saw the way Edward was looking at her, with a strange half-smile on his lips and a darkness in his eyes.

'The wine's brought a flush to your skin,' he said softly.

But it wasn't the wine. It was the way he was looking at her. It was the way she felt, watching him. It was...

She shoved back her chair and stood up. 'It's—it's getting late,' she said. 'And we have to talk.'

It took a moment before he nodded. 'All right.' He rose and walked across the room. 'Let's have a brandy and go out on the terrace.'

'No.' Olivia shook her head as he turned towards her. 'I have to be leaving soon, Edward. Tomorrow's a working day for me. I only came here so I could tell you that—that... The thing is, I wasn't entirely honest with you last night. I mean, when you asked me——'

He looked at her. 'I asked you a lot of things last night.'

Their eyes met, and suddenly the atmosphere changed. Olivia touched the tip of her tongue to her lips.

'I asked you if a man had ever licked champagne from the hollow between your breasts.' His voice was soft. 'Do you remember? It was all I could think of after I left you, what it would be like to touch my mouth to your flesh.'

Her heart raced as he came towards her. His arms encircled her, drawing her close to the heat of his body. She wanted to break away, but it was impossible. She was powerless, held not only by his arms but by her own need.

'Let me taste you tonight, Olivia.'

He bent and touched his tongue to her mouth, lightly tracing the outline of her lips, and they parted.

'No,' she whispered, 'Edward, you mustn't.'

'I must,' he said, sounding like a man in torment. His hand slipped into her hair, tilted her head back and held her fast. '*We* must, Olivia. What's the sense in trying to deny it?'

His mouth swooped down on hers, hot and hungry, and she made a whimpering sound in the back of her throat.

'Put your arms around me,' he whispered against her lips.

Her hands slipped up his chest and curled tightly around his neck, her fingers thrusting deep into the dark hair that lay just above his collar. She moaned softly at the feel of it, silken and soft as she had known it would be.

Edward's hands slid down her back; he lifted her to her toes so that her hips pressed tightly against his. The evidence of his arousal pressed against her.

'I want you,' he whispered.

And she wanted him. Oh, yes, she wanted to be with him, to kiss him as she'd never kissed another man, to hold him tightly in her arms until his heartbeat and hers were one. It made no sense, she knew that. But this wasn't about sense, it was about senses. It was about the sweetness of his mouth, the warmth of his breath; about the heat of the little kisses he pressed on the sensitive skin behind her ear. He licked the hollow of her throat where her pulse beat an excited tattoo, then slipped his hands under her shirt. She made a soft sound as he cupped her breasts; she felt her nipples thrusting against the flimsy silk of her bra, as if seeking his unimpeded touch.

'Olivia.'

Edward's hands were at the fastener of her jeans. She heard the soft click of the press-stud, the faint snick of the zip as he drew it open...

God. Oh, God, what was she doing? This was what he'd expected of her all along, this—this easy acquiescence. It was what men always expected—and what she never delivered. She had always met groping hands and damp mouths with a natural frigidity that was more effective than any slap, yet here she was, clinging to this man who was her enemy, moving her hips against his, matching his insane kisses with her own.

'I'm the only man who can make you feel what you've been faking for so long...'

The memory of his ugly words returned her to sanity. She went still in his arms, and her hands flattened on his chest.

'That's enough,' she said, her voice as cold as her face.

Edward blinked. 'What?' he said, his eyes fogged with desire.

'I mean, you can't blame me for wondering how far you'd go, Edward. Now I know.' She smiled mirthlessly. 'I'm just not sure what it is you're after. Do you want what your stepfather had? Or is it Ria's address?'

His face twisted, his eyes glinting with such sudden rage that it struck terror into her heart. His hands slid to her wrists, tightened until it was all she could do not to cry out at the steely bite of his fingers.

'You bitch,' he said thickly. 'I ought to——'

'What? Beat me?' Olivia forced her eyes to meet his. 'That won't get you what you want, either.'

'Why not? How do I know you wouldn't enjoy it?'

One hard, fast slap to his face was all she managed. He caught her wrist while her hand was still in the air, and she cried out as he twisted her arm behind her and drew her towards him.

'That's twice,' he said through his teeth. 'The third time, you'll have to pay the piper.'

'Isn't it enough that I've been with you this evening?' she said coldly.

He glared at her, his breathing hard and fast, and then he all but flung her from him.

'I'll call down to the doorman. He'll have a taxi waiting by the time you reach the lobby.'

She turned on her heel and made her way from the room. She was stepping into the lift when the sound of her name made her look back. Edward had followed her as far as the living-room. He stood in the wide archway, silhouetted against the wall of windows, dark and tall and dangerous.

'What is it?' she said.

'We still haven't talked.'

'We have nothing to say to each other.'

He took a step forward. 'I said I wanted to see you. Don't you want to know why?'

Her laughter took all the courage she possessed. 'I'm not stupid, Edward.'

'Olivia, about Ria——'

'If Ria ever asks my advice, I'm going to tell her to take that stock and run.'

Her heart leaped as he moved quickly towards her, but she slapped her hand against the control panel. The door slid shut in his face, and Olivia collapsed back against the wall.

CHAPTER SIX

THE only good thing about what had happened in Edward's apartment, Olivia thought late the next morning, was that it meant she would never see him again. She'd rebuffed his advances, insulted him, assured him that she would never urge Ria to return the stock he so badly wanted—no, she thought as she sat in her living-room, sipping a cup of rapidly cooling coffee, she would not have to deal with Edward Archer any more.

And it was a good thing, too. Her life was in enough turmoil without having to deal with him. The arrogant bastard! Just who did he think he was?

Olivia got to her feet and stalked to the kitchen. *She* knew who he was, or at least she knew *what* he was, she thought as she slammed her cup down on the sink. He was a man who didn't give a damn about anything or anyone but himself, a man willing to use her to get what he wanted.

But then, she was expendable. As far as Edward was concerned, she was little better than a tramp who'd slept with his stepfather, a slut who knew where to find Ria Bascomb but stubbornly refused to tell him.

She shut off the water and dried her hands on a towel. It didn't matter why he'd tried to seduce her, whether it was out of some twisted sense of *machismo* or because he'd hoped for some indiscreet 'pillow talk' that would put him on Ria's trail. All that counted was that he'd humiliated her again—and she'd helped him do it.

Her cheeks flamed as she remembered how she'd responded to his kisses. It only proved just how topsy-turvy her world had become. Early this morning, she'd made the toughest decision of her life. She'd closed the shop.

'Just for a couple of weeks,' she'd assured Dulcie, and the other girl had smiled gently and assured her that she knew it wouldn't be for long.

But it might well be forever, and they both knew it. There hadn't been a customer inside the place since the scandal had broken, and, without customers, Olivia's Dream would soon be dead.

And it was Ria's fault. Ria, who was still among the missing. Ria, who'd started all this yet remained untouched by gossip.

Olivia grimaced. 'If I knew where you were, Ria,' she muttered, 'I'd grab you by the shoulders and shake you till your teeth rattled!'

Her shoulders sagged, and she walked slowly to the window and put her palms on the sill as she looked out. If she knew where Ria was, she wouldn't be stuck away up here while her business fell to pieces, she wouldn't be...

Her breath hissed. Edward Archer was stepping briskly from his car and striding towards the shop. He was wearing a leather jacket, faded jeans, and low leather boots, and he looked as if anything that got in his way would be in for trouble.

She shrank back as he cast a grimly assessing glance at the windows of her flat. Her heart was racing, but that was ridiculous. He couldn't see her. And he couldn't get up here. He'd have to stand in the street and ring the shop bell.

And she wouldn't answer it. He'd have to give up, eventually, he'd have to go away.

But he didn't. He rang and rang, and when she finally heard his fist slam against the wood Olivia muttered an oath and flew across the room. Her bare feet pounded on the steps as she raced downstairs and hurtled through the shop. Her fingers flew over the bolts and then she wrenched the door open.

'Go away,' she demanded, her upturned face flushed with indignation.

Edward's expression gave nothing away. 'Hello, Olivia. Aren't you going to ask me in?'

'No.' She was breathing hard, fairly shaking with rage. She slapped her hands on her hips and stared at him in defiance. 'I am not going to do any such thing.'

His gaze moved over her and a slow flush heated her body as she realised how she must look in her long flannel robe, with her hair undone and her bare toes peeking out beneath her hem. The robe covered her from throat to ankle, yet the way he looked at her made her feel exposed. Still, she stood her ground. To do anything else would somehow signal defeat.

'I take it you're not opening the shop today,' he said.

Olivia smiled tightly. 'What a brilliant deduction. Are you always this clever so early in the morning?'

'I have to talk to you.'

'Yes. That's what you said last night,' she said as she started to shut the door. 'But I don't want to talk to *you*.'

'Believe me, I wouldn't have come here if I had any choice.'

'I'll bet! I'll just——' The door slapped back as he shouldered his way past her. 'Hey! *Hey*! Where do you think you're going?'

'Inside,' he said grimly. 'Unlike you, I've no desire to find our conversation recorded for posterity in the pages of the *Chatterbox*.'

Olivia caught her lip between her teeth. In her anger, she'd forgotten the reporters that had begun to appear at odd hours outside the shop. But a quick glance showed the street was mercifully empty, and she threw caution to the wind.

'Oh, I don't know,' she said, tossing her head. 'I'd think this would make a particularly fascinating story for the *Chatterbox*. "Stepson Follows in Stepfather's Footsteps."' She frowned. 'No. No, that's far too clumsy to make a good headline. But you get the general idea. Think of how many newspapers they'll sell if they do a

piece on you, on how you found your way straight to
the door of the woman the papers say was your stepfather's——'

She gasped as his hands went around her waist and
he lifted her inside, then slammed the door shut.

'You can't do this,' she huffed. 'Dammit, you can't
just storm in here and——'

'You're going to lose Olivia's Dream.'

It was a flat statement, delivered with such assurance
that it silenced her more effectively than a slap.

'What do you mean?'

'Just what I said. You've lost your customers, and
now you've closed the shop.'

'It's temporary,' she said quickly.

'Sure.' His smile was chill. 'The way the bubonic
plague was temporary. How will you pay your bills?'
His smile twisted. 'This month's loan payment, for instance. You haven't made it, but, of course, you're not
worried about that. Good old Charlie forgave it.'

She ignored his sarcastic comment. 'The *Chatterbox*
can't keep the story going forever,' she said with more
conviction than she felt. 'As soon as business picks up...'

'How can business pick up if the shop is closed?' He
folded his arms across his chest. 'Even with Wright's
generous "gift",' Edward said softly, 'you're still verging
on bankruptcy. What do you say, Olivia? Do you want
to talk—or do you want to sulk?'

Olivia glared at him. 'I can't imagine what we could
possibly have to talk about.'

'Our mutual problem.' His lips drew back from his
teeth. 'Ria Bascomb.'

He was right about that. Ria held the key to
everything.

She lifted her chin. 'You have two minutes.'

'You want to talk here?' He laughed unpleasantly. 'For
all I know, the *Chatterbox* has this place wired.'

She paled. 'Don't be ridiculous.' Their eyes met. 'All
right. Give me ten minutes to dress.'

Edward smiled thinly. 'Make it five.'

'Or what?' Pride made her stubborn.

His smile was suddenly sexy and taut with dangerous promise. 'Do you really want to find out?'

Colour rose in her cheeks. There had to be something she could say that would put him in his place—but it seemed far safer to beat a quick, if not hasty, retreat.

Once she was safely in her flat, she moved quickly, slipping into corduroy trousers, an ivory bulky knit sweater, and a pair of well-worn jogging shoes. She went into the bathroom and looked into the mirror as she brushed back her dark hair, securing it at the crown with a tortoiseshell clasp. Her hand went automatically towards the drawer where she kept her make-up, but then she drew it back. No. No make-up, not even a discreet whisk of mascara or lipstick, not for this encounter with a man she hated. She pulled her anorak from the closet, and she was ready.

He was waiting when she came down the stairs, leaning against the wall, hands tucked into his pockets, feet crossed at the ankles.

'Well?' she said, her voice tinged with defiance. 'Are you satisfied?'

His gaze moved over her slowly, and when his eyes finally met hers, there was a curious light in their dark depths.

'Yes,' he said softly. 'Very.' He continued to look at her while the seconds ticked by, and then, suddenly, a cool mask seemed to click over his face. 'Let's go,' he said briskly, and he turned and made his way swiftly to the door.

She had no idea where he was heading, and she didn't much care. If he knew of some quiet spot where there was no risk of someone recognising her, she was all for it.

They crossed the George Washington Bridge leading out of the city and the car picked up some speed once they were free of traffic. Edward drove with competence and skill, just a little faster than he should have. It was, somehow, exactly as Olivia had known he'd drive on this narrow, winding road that followed the bank of the Hudson River.

She glanced up from beneath the sweep of her lashes. They were seated close together, close enough so his leather-gloved knuckles had grazed her leg once when he changed gears. A tingling sensation had run along her nerve-endings at that light touch and she'd held herself stiffly after that, staying as far away from him as she could. But his shoulder still occasionally brushed hers, and the scent of his light, clean cologne was in her nostrils.

The faint shadow of a dark beard lay smudged across his chin and cheekbones. It lent a hard look to his face. No. Not hard. He looked—he looked strong and very masculine. Her eyes went to his hands, lying lightly on the steering-wheel, and she suddenly remembered the feel of those long fingers on her skin, the heat of his touch...

A choked sound escaped her throat and she twisted in her seat and stared out the windscreen.

Edward glanced at her. 'Did you say something?'

'I—I...' She swallowed. 'I just wondered when we'd get to our talk.'

'Soon. There's a place just ahead.' He swung the wheel to the right. 'Here we are.'

He slowed the car as they drove into a deserted car park. A narrow gravel path marked 'trailhead' curved sinuously into a stand of tall pines before vanishing from view.

'What is this place?' Olivia asked as he shut off the engine.

He smiled. 'The best place I know of when you need privacy.'

She undid her seatbelt and followed him out of the car. 'Because you can spot the reporters a mile away?'

His smile became a grin. 'Because it's peaceful and beautiful, and a *Chatterbox* reporter would probably rather die than follow us into the woods.'

He was right, Olivia thought as they walked slowly into the sheltering forest, it *was* peaceful in here, and beautiful. The dark green of the tall trees seemed almost to pierce the winter-blue sky, the breeze was muted and carried the crisp tang of pine.

Edward seemed very much at home, strolling along with a steady, even stride, offering his hand to her when a deadfall blocked the way. And yet, she'd never have imagined him in a setting like this. The Edward Archer she knew belonged in his penthouse, high above the city, or in a leather-lined corporate boardroom, not here with the wind ruffling his hair the way she had ruffled it the other night. The memory was almost palpable.

'... of the city?'

She looked at him. They'd come out on the shore of a pond rimmed with tall marsh grasses. Edward was leaning back against the trunk of a tree, watching her.

'Sorry. Did you ask me a question?'

He bent and picked up a flat stone. 'I said, do you ever get out of Manhattan?' He flung back his arm and tossed the stone, watching as it skipped lightly across the water before sinking beneath the surface. 'Or are you strictly a city girl?'

Olivia's head came up sharply. Was there a subtle kind of insult in the seemingly innocent words? But he wasn't even looking at her. He'd scooped up a handful of the small stones and now he was skipping them across the pond, watching the concentric rings they left as they touched the water.

'I like the country,' she said slowly. 'But I don't get the chance to get away very often.'

'When I was a kid, I used to wait all year for the summer,' Edward said. 'It meant we'd go to our house in Connecticut. My father was alive then; he used to take me fishing with him.' He smiled. 'We never caught much, but that didn't seem to matter.'

Olivia smiled, too. 'I only went fishing once, and it wasn't very successful. I wouldn't bait the hook, and neither would Ria. She...'

Her words faded away. Ria. Ria was the reason she and Edward were here. Somehow, she'd almost forgotten that.

'You were childhood friends?' he asked softly, watching her.

She nodded. 'Yes. I was ten and she was eleven when we met.'

'School chums?'

'No. Not at all.' She looked directly at him. 'My parents died when I was ten, and I went to live with my Great-Aunt Miriam.' She paused. 'She was the Bascombs' housekeeper.'

Edward's eyes narrowed. 'I see.'

'Do you?' Her hackles were up again; she had seen that calculating look too many times in her life not to recognise it.

'Yes. Ria Bascomb befriended you when you most needed her. It explains why you've felt such a determined need to protect her.'

Olivia turned away. 'It's what friends do,' she said stiffly.

'Ria doesn't seem to subscribe to that philosophy.'

'Well, she—she's upset. Charles's death...'

'It couldn't have upset her any more than it upset you.'

'I was sorry to hear about it, of course, but——'

'I suppose, in a sense, it's commendable that you felt a sentimental attachment to Wright and not just a—how shall I put it? A "business" interest.'

She felt the swift rise of colour in her cheeks as she swung towards him.

'You're as bad as the papers,' she said tightly. 'You don't know a damned thing about me, but you're more than willing to jump to the worst possible conclusions. People like you——'

Edward caught hold of her arms. '*Did* you care about him?' he said roughly.

'Yes. Of course. But not——'

'But not what?' His grasp tightened. 'Not enough to see past his chequebook?'

'Dammit, Edward, I never——'

'No. You never. Never stopped to think that he was just a dirty old man, who had no more right to touch you than—than...' He fell silent, his beathing harsh and ragged, his eyes dark with condemnation, and then his hands fell away from her. 'You're correct,' he said coldly. 'I've no right to judge you.'

Olivia turned her back to him and blinked back the sudden sharp bite of tears.

'No,' she said. 'You haven't.'

She heard him puff out his breath. 'We came here to talk,' he said. 'Perhaps we'd better get to it.'

She nodded. 'Maybe we had.'

Edward clasped her shoulder and turned her towards him. 'I want you to help me find Ria Bascomb.'

'You mean, you're not going to insist I know where she is?'

He shook his head. 'I know you don't.'

'How?' Her smile was bitter. 'Is it my honest face?'

He hesitated. 'I had you watched.'

'What?' Her mouth dropped open. 'You—you had me——'

'Did you think we were playing children's games, Olivia?' His expression turn grim. 'I want that stock.'

'And you'll do anything to get it! I suppose it's worth a fortune.'

A tight smile curved across his mouth. 'I suppose you could say that, yes.'

'Well?' Her face flushed with barely controlled anger. 'What did your detective say about me? Besides the fact that Ria hasn't been slipping in and out of my flat, I mean?'

A moment of silence passed before Edward spoke. 'He said that you don't seem to have replaced old Charlie,' he said softly.

'Really.' Her voice shook with anger. 'Are you sure? After all, no one's checked under my bed.'

A muscle worked in his jaw. 'Why haven't you? Is it because you don't need a new benefactor just yet?'

'I don't need a benefactor at all,' she said, spitting the word out with contempt. 'I take care of myself.'

'In fact, the detective told me there doesn't seem to be a man in your life at all.' Edward's gaze swept over her face, lingering on her parted lips. 'And I find that difficult to believe.'

'Did you bring me out here to insult me?'

'You need a man's hands on your skin.' Edward's voice grew soft and husky as he framed her face in his hands. His thumbs swept lazily across her cheekbones. 'You're as soft as silk,' he whispered. He lowered his head and buried his face in her hair. 'And you smell like flowers.' He drew back just enough so he could look into her eyes. 'Do you smell that way all over, Olivia? Your breasts, your belly, the soft, sweet darkness between your thighs?'

Her breath caught. 'You,' she gasped, 'you—you...'

A low laugh rumbled in his throat. 'That's right, darling. Me. No one but me.' He bent and kissed her before she could pull away, his mouth moving over hers hungrily. When finally he let her go, she was trembling.

'Why *did* you bring me here?' she whispered.

Edward stared at her, saying nothing for a long moment, and then he drew a deep breath and turned to the pond again.

'I've a proposition to offer you.' His voice was cool, as if what had just happened between them had never occurred.

A proposition. Olivia wrapped her arms around herself.

'I suppose I should be flattered, Edward.' She knew she sounded calm and in control, even though his words had sent a bitter taste flooding into her mouth. Hearing herself gave her the courage to go on. 'Especially since you made such a brave speech about not following in your stepfather's footsteps. But I'm afraid I'm not interested.'

He swung around and gave her a cold smile. 'I'm sorry to disappoint you, Olivia, but this is strictly a business proposition. I'll agree to pay your bills until this mess quietens down and, in return, you'll help me locate Ria.'

Olivia laughed. 'And I always thought the standard fee was thirty pieces of silver.'

'Be as clever as you like,' he snapped. 'All the quips in the world won't give you back your reputation. Your public one, anyway. Only Ria can do that.'

He was right, of course. She knew he was right, and only a fool would pretend otherwise.

She wanted to cry with the injustice of it, to shout out her anger at this man who had turned her life upside-down. She wanted to scrub her hand across her mouth and wipe away the taste of his kiss. But it was the bottom line that counted in the real world. She needed to find Ria if she was going to keep her life from falling apart.

And so she drew herself up and steadily met his gaze.

'You can *lend* me the money at current interest rates.'

'I said I'd give it to you.'

Olivia squared her shoulders. 'It's a loan, or the deal's off.'

Edward smiled slightly. 'You're not in a position where you can set the rules, darling.'

'Take it or leave it,' she said.

She watched his face, waiting for anger to darken his eyes. What she saw in them mystified her, but it was gone before she could even try to identify it.

'All right,' he said briskly, 'Have it your way.' He took her arm and they began walking along the narrow path that followed the contour of the pond, his touch firm and impersonal. 'I've been going through Wright's personal effects. He left a paper trail a mile wide: hotel receipts, airline tickets, theatre stubs...'

'What has that to do with finding Ria?'

'You know her,' he said. 'The things she likes, the places she prefers... I want you to go through Wright's papers and see if something strikes a bell. A hotel, a hideaway—some place she's mentioned in the past where she might have gone to ground.'

They had circled the pond and come out into the parking area again. Their heels crunched across the gravel as they walked towards Edward's car.

'You just told me you'd hired a private detective,' Olivia said. 'Isn't what you're describing a job for him?'

'Not when you're the one who knows her habits. You're her friend.'

Was she? A friend wouldn't do what Edward was proposing—but then, a friend wouldn't do what Ria had done to her, either. A friend wouldn't have left her so utterly, terribly alone.

'Well?' He caught her arm and turned her to face him. 'Will you do it?'

Olivia hesitated, and then she took a deep breath. 'Why are you asking? I don't have any choice.'

'No,' he said, 'you don't.' He opened the door and she stepped into the car. He came around, slid in beside her, and started the engine. Silence grew between them as he drove out of the car park and swung on to the road. After a long while, he glanced over at her. 'We'll start going through Wright's things tonight, at my apartment.'

Tonight. At Edward's apartment.

'Do you have a problem with that?' he asked.

She waited, listening to the sound of the tyres and to the suddenly erratic beat of her heart, and then she shook her head and put her head back against the seat.

'No. No, not at all.'

Edward waited, too; she could feel his burning gaze moving over her profile, lingering for a heated moment on her mouth, and then he turned and stared straight out through the windscreen.

'Good girl,' he said softly.

He put his foot down on the accelerator, and the car shot ahead.

CHAPTER SEVEN

EDWARD'S wood-panelled study was quiet, save for the soft hiss of flame from the logs blazing in the fieldstone fireplace and the sweet strains of Debussy playing softly in the background.

Olivia was seated on a low black loveseat before the fire, her stockinged feet tucked up beneath her as she leafed through a stack of receipts and bills lying in her lap. Every few moments, she disposed of another one, tossing it to the floor where it joined the other discards.

A log tumbled into the fire and she looked up, startled by the sound. Her glance flew to Edward, who was sitting in a wing-back chair, head back, eyes closed, hands lying loosely on the chair's arms.

How weary he looked. There were dark smudges beneath his eyes, and a faint hollowing under his high cheekbones. His mouth was curved down at the corners.

She was weary, too. It had been a long day. And a difficult one. They'd made the drive back in silence. By the time they'd reached Manhattan, Olivia had been counting the moments until she was safely alone in her flat.

But Edward had not driven her there. Instead, he'd headed further east, towards the river, towards Sutton Place, and it wasn't until he'd pulled to the kerb and shut off the engine that she'd realised where he'd brought her.

Somewhere inside this grey building overlooking the East River was the flat the *Chatterbox* had so inelegantly labelled 'Wright's Love Nest'.

Olivia swung towards him. 'What are we doing here?' she demanded.

His smile was cool. 'I thought there might be some odds and ends worth going through tucked away in your little hideaway.'

'My little . . .'

'Come along, darling.' Edward undid his seatbelt and reached for the door handle. 'We'll take a quick look, and——'

'I don't want to go in there,' she said quickly.

'Are you afraid of the photographers? Don't be. The Press finished with this place a week ago.'

Olivia turned away and stared out of the windscreen. 'I want to go home.'

'Seeing the flat again reminds you of what you've lost, does it?' He caught hold of her wrist. 'Look at me, dammit!'

'Don't bully me, Edward. I don't like it.'

His lips drew back from his teeth. 'I'll just bet you don't. Old Charlie was your kind of man, happy to pay the bills just so you'd be waiting, warm and willing, in his bed.'

'Let go!'

His head bent towards her. 'How warm and willing were you?' His gaze moved over her face and lingered on her parted lips. 'Did you make those soft little sounds that drive a man crazy, the way you do when I make love to you?'

'You've never made love to——'

'No,' he said, and suddenly his voice was soft and filled with promise, not anger. The press of his hand on hers changed; she felt the slow stroke of his thumb against her pulse. 'I haven't. But I will.' Their eyes met. 'You know I will.'

It was a moment that called for a clever one-liner, something that would deflate his ego and assert hers, but it was as if his words, his very presence, held her transfixed. Olivia could feel his breath, see the pulse beating in his temple, and she knew that she had only to whisper his name for his mouth to come down on hers...

Edward let go of her, turned away sharply, and wrapped his hands tightly around the steering-wheel.

'Never mind,' he said, as calmly as if nothing had happened. 'I've been through the whole flat twice, I doubt if I've missed anything important.'

Olivia folded her hands in her lap. They were trembling, and she laced her fingers tightly together.

'Is that where you got the papers you want me to see?'

He nodded as he pulled out into traffic. 'Some of them, yes. I'll send a cab for you this evening. Be ready at seven o'clock.'

She looked at his harsh, implacable profile, the outthrust jaw and straight nose, and suddenly she wished to heaven she'd never agreed to meet with him tonight or to the bargain they'd made.

It was too late to try and back out of their agreement. Edward would give her no peace if she did. But it wasn't too late to assert herself.

'Seven's no good,' she'd said coolly. 'We'll make it half-past. And I'll get my own cab, thank you.'

There had been a moment's silence, and then, to her surprise, Edward had laughed.

'Just be on time, darling,' he'd said. 'I don't like my women to keep me waiting.'

It had taken effort not to remind him that she was not one of his women, but Olivia had been smart enough to know that answering a remark like that would only have led to trouble.

Still, she'd been uncertain what kind of mood Edward would be in when she arrived at his apartment hours later, but he'd treated her with punctilious courtesy from the second she'd arrived.

She glanced at him now. Why wouldn't he? He wanted information from her. He wasn't about to insult her. Olivia sighed as she glanced at the papers lying on the floor next to her. But it had all been for nothing. She'd pored over every hotel bill, every restaurant receipt, and she still hadn't a clue as to where Ria might have gone.

'No luck.'

She looked up. Edward was watching her, his face expressionless.

She shook her head. 'None. I've gone through all this stuff twice, just to be certain, but I don't remember ever hearing Ria mention any of these places.'

'Are you sure?'

'As sure as I can be, considering the circumstances.'

'Meaning?'

Olivia sat forward and pushed her hands through her hair, combing through the dark strands with her fingers.

'Meaning I wasn't taking notes each time I spoke to her.'

'And none of those names means anything to you.'

'I thought that's what I said.' She looked at him as he rose and walked to the fireplace. 'What is it, Edward? Do you think I'm lying?'

He shrugged as he took the poker from the hearth. 'I didn't say that.'

'No. You didn't. But from the look on your face——'

He bent forward and prodded one of the logs. Sparks shimmered into the updraught and vanished up the flue.

'Where did he take you, then?'

She blinked. 'What?'

'It's a simple question, Olivia.' He set aside the poker and turned to face her. The scowl was gone, and in its place was a grim mask. 'It just occurs to me that you and he must have special places you went to together, inns or little hideaways upstate somewhere... What are you doing?'

'I'm getting ready to go home,' she said coldly. 'It's been a long day, and I'm exhausted.'

'I'm not trying to pry——'

'No. You're trying to insult me.' She looked at him. 'And you're succeeding.'

104   A WOMAN ACCUSED

Edward spread his hands. 'I only meant that perhaps he'd taken Ria somewhere he'd taken you.'

'I'm sure he did,' she said, even more coldly. She waited a moment, and then she gave him a chilly smile. 'That restaurant in the Village, the one the *Chatterbox* insisted was the scene of endless assignations, for instance. They served terrific Sicilian pizza there, and Ria loves pizza.' Olivia got to her feet. 'It's a pretty good bet that that's one of the places he took her.'

Edward met her gaze levelly. 'Undoubtedly. So, you're suggesting Ria is hiding in a vat of marinara sauce.'

'No. I——' She looked at him. There was a hint of laughter in his eyes, and after a few seconds she smiled reluctantly. 'Well, it's a thought. At least it would explain how someone could just vanish into thin air.'

He sank down on the raised edge of the hearth and stretched his long legs out in front of him.

'No one does, except in bad films.' He leaned back on his elbows and crossed his legs at the ankle. 'OK, then. I'll have the detective agency check out those places anyway. But we're going to have to try another approach.'

Olivia sighed wearily. 'When you come up with something,' she said, 'let me know.' She bent forward, her long hair swinging forward to veil her face as she slipped on her shoes. 'Just do me a favour, please, and phone down to the doorman for a cab so I can——'

'What kinds of things does she like?'

She paused. 'What kinds of things...?'

'Is she athletic? Does she like winter sports—skiing, skating, that sort of stuff?'

Olivia thought for a moment. 'No,' she said slowly, 'at least, she never did when we were kids.'

'What about the arts?' Edward leaned towards the sofa and scooped up a brochure with the picture of a violin on its cover. 'This is about a music festival in Aspen— would she have been interested in something like that?'

'Ria?' She smiled. 'I doubt it.'

'But she works in a gallery...?'

'Well, it's the trendy thing to...' Olivia bit her lip. She knew, in her heart, that it was the truth. Ria was like that. But it was hard enough to admit such things about Ria to herself, let alone to anyone else. 'I mean, she—she took some art courses in college.'

Edward's face was without expression. 'And you? Is that what lured you into decorating? The fact that it's "trendy"?'

Olivia's eyes flashed. 'There's nothing trendy about decorating.'

'Isn't there?' He snatched up the rest of the papers, walked to a desk on the far wall, and dumped them into an open drawer. 'The customer who goes into Olivia's Dream isn't very likely to do the rest of her shopping at a discount store.'

'Neither is the customer who goes to Edward Archer for—what is it you do, Edward? Sell stocks and bonds because it's "trendy" in your circle?'

His brows rose. 'I'm an arbitrageur,' he said tightly, 'and a damned good one. I am *not* a sales...' A slow smile spread across his face, softening its harshness. '*Touché*. My apologies, darling.'

A flush rose along her cheekbones. 'And I wish you wouldn't call me that.'

Edward looked at her. 'All right,' he said easily, after what seemed like a long silence. 'I won't.'

She nodded. 'Thank you.' Her voice was taut.

'You're welcome.'

She looked up quickly, but the taunting smile she'd expected to see wasn't there. Instead, he was watching her with a sudden intensity that made her breathing quicken. She turned away.

'Is that it, then?' she said. 'Are we done playing twenty questions for the night?'

'Yes,' he said finally, 'I guess we are. It's late. I've hounded you enough for one day.'

'In that case...' She rose to her feet. 'Would you call down to the lobby and arrange for a cab? And if you should think of anything about Ria...'

'To hell with Ria!'

The anger in his voice caught her by surprise. She stared at him.

'What do you mean, to hell with Ria?'

'Just what I said.' Edward's eyes glittered. 'I'm sick of hearing her name, sick of thinking about that bastard Wright and his dirty little games, sick of...' His lips clamped together and he rubbed his hand across his forehead. 'You're right,' he said after a long silence. 'It *has* been a long day.'

Olivia nodded. 'Yes. That's why I'm leav——'

'What we need is a drink.'

A drink. A drink was what he'd offered her in this same apartment just the other night, and then he'd taken her in his arms and kissed her until she was dizzy with—with...

'Olivia? What would you like?'

'Nothing,' she said quickly. 'I'd fall on my face if I had anything stronger than a cup of coffee, and——'

'Coffee sounds great.' Edward smiled easily. 'In fact, it sounds terrific, considering that my houseman's not here.'

Olivia's brows rose. 'Are you telling me you don't drink coffee if he's not here to make it?'

'Only instant,' he said with an exaggerated grimace. His smile became a lopsided grin. 'Don't look at me like that.'

'I can't believe it. This is the dawn of the twenty-first century. Hasn't anyone told you that men are no longer barred from the kitchen?'

'Hey, I can scramble a mean egg. And I can grill a steak. I even know enough to tear the lettuce leaves for a salad instead of cutting them.' He smiled. 'But I can't make a cup of coffee worth the name.'

She wanted to smile back at him. In fact, it took concentrated effort not to. He looked relaxed and engaging, less like the enemy than the boy next door.

And that was just the point. The boy next door *was* the enemy, he always had been, only now he was twice as dangerous, an adult male, handsome and potent.

'I was in college the last time I made coffee.' He chuckled. 'My roommate made me take off my shoes so he could be sure I hadn't used my socks to brew it.'

Olivia's mouth twitched. 'That's really tragic.'

Edward nodded. 'It is, especially when I've got a perfectly good Chemex and fresh coffee beans in the kitchen.'

She looked at him for a long moment. What was there to fear in a cup of coffee? Besides, he was right. Coffee would be perfect, it would wipe away the cobwebs.

'All kinds of coffee beans,' he added hopefully.

'I suppose you have a coffee grinder, too?'

Edward smiled. 'Electric or crank-the-handle? You get your choice.'

This time, she permitted herself a small smile in return. 'You mean, you get yours. You grind, I brew. Deal?'

He held his hand out to her. She hesitated, then gave herself a brisk mental shake.

'Deal.' A handshake was only a handshake, after all.

Then why did her fingers tingle as if she'd touched high-voltage wire?

It was, as she might have expected, a handsome and very well equipped kitchen, and Edward hadn't exaggerated when he said he had all sorts of beans. There was half a freezer shelf of foil-wrapped packets, each bearing the name of some exotic place.

'Brazil,' Olivia murmured, 'Kenya, Colombia, Java...'

'Have you ever had coffee from Hawaii?' he asked. She shook her head and he reached past her, his body brushing lightly against hers. The tingle surged through her again, even more sharply. She must have reacted in

some way—a quick breath, a little tremor, something
that gave her away—because he turned and gave her a
searching look.

'What is it?'

Their eyes met. 'Nothing,' she said. 'I just...' She
swallowed and turned her back to him. 'Where's the
coffee-pot?'

It was in the cupboard over the sink, along with a
stack of paper filters and an assortment of handsome
mugs. The simple procedures that came next were more
than welcome—rinsing the glass flask, filling the kettle
with water and setting it on to boil while the coffee
grinder whirred in the background—all of it tethered her
skittish emotions to reality. By the time Edward handed
over the finely ground coffee beans, Olivia felt herself
again.

'That's it,' he said gravely. 'If I do anything more, I'll
only contaminate the process. From now on, *madame*,
the entire procedure is in your hands.'

She smiled. 'Stand back, then, and let a true artist
work.'

When she'd finished measuring the roasted grounds
into the filter, she turned to find Edward straddling one
of the high-backed stools that stood at the end of the
long Formica counter. His arms were draped over the
back and his chin rested lightly on his tanned forearms.

'Is that what you wanted to be when you grew up?
An artist?'

She looked puzzled for a moment, and then she
laughed. 'Me?'

'Yeah. Did you want to be the next Marc Chagall
before you decided to become an interior decorator?'

'I thought about sculpting,' she said without thinking.
She cleared her throat and looked at him. 'I mean, I
did, a long time ago. But——'

'But?'

She shrugged her shoulders. 'But I don't have the
talent. Oh, I can do nice little pieces: puppies, sleeping

cats, figures, that sort of stuff, but I could never do important things.'

'Ah.' He smiled. 'You gave up because you couldn't reproduce Michelangelo's *David*. Well, not many artists can.'

She smiled, too. 'No, of course they can't. I didn't mean that. I meant that I can't do good sculptures, pieces that make a difference in people's lives, that—that...' Her voice faded. No one, not even Ria or her great-aunt, had ever asked her if she'd harboured a serious dream about art. And yet this man, this stranger who had intruded himself into her life, had thought to ask it—and she had answered, she, who never gave anything of herself away to anyone.

'What's the matter?'

'Nothing,' she said, swinging away from him. 'I—I thought I heard the water starting to boil.'

'It whistles.'

'What?'

'The kettle. It whistles when it's ready.' She heard the stool scrape and the soft pad of his footsteps. A little tremor ran along her spine as he came up beside her. 'Here,' he said, 'I'll do that.' Her shoulder brushed hers as he leaned past her. 'So, you never thought of making a career sculpting those little figures?'

Why was it so hard to breathe? Olivia cleared her throat. 'What—what little figures?'

'Puppies and sleeping cats.' Edward leaned back against the counter, arms crossed over his chest, his eyes on her face. 'Someone must, after all.'

Why had she agreed to make coffee? Why didn't the damned kettle whistle? Why was he standing so close?

'Must—must what?' she said stupidly.

'Must make all those awful little statues you see at tourist stands, the ones that say "Souvenir of Podunk".'

'Do you—do you take milk and sugar?'

'Black is fine.'

'And the napkins. Where are they?'

'I'll get them.' She breathed out a sigh of relief as he moved away. 'Couldn't you have made a living making chubby-cheeked babies, puppies, and kitsch?'

'Yes,' she said, 'I suppose. But——'

'But what?'

'Well, it's not—it's not for me. There's nothing wrong with doing that sort of thing. But it just seems, I don't know, a sham to study art and then turn out cookie-cutter stuff like that.' She gave an embarrassed laugh. 'That sounds pretentious, doesn't it? I didn't mean to——'

'It sounds honest.'

His voice was soft, but it seemed to carry the length of the room. She turned and looked at him, and what she saw in his eyes sent her pulse racing.

'Olivia,' he said softly, and just then the kettle gave a piercing shriek.

The breath rushed from her lungs. 'That's enough to wake the dead,' she said with a little laugh, and she turned away and busied herself with formalities of brewing the coffee.

Edward pronounced it excellent after the first sip. 'Is there a school for coffee making?' he said, flashing her an ingratiating grin. 'One that I've missed all these years?'

She smiled back at him over the rim of her cup. 'I've no idea. I learned whatever I know from Mrs Fanning.'

'A home economics teacher in high school?'

'The Bascombs' cook.' Olivia wrinkled her nose. 'Pardon me. Their chef.'

His brows rose mockingly. 'Do I detect a note of disdain, Miss Harris?'

'Oh, it wasn't Mrs Fanning who called herself that, it was Mrs Bascomb.' Olivia made a face. 'She was— is—a very proper lady.'

Edward put down his cup. 'It must have been rough, settling into the Bascomb household,' he said, his eyes on hers.

She shrugged. 'A little.'

'Were you and your aunt close?'

'No. We hardly knew each other when my parents died, and...' Olivia fell silent. Why was she telling him all this? Surely he wasn't interested in hearing the story of her life. She looked at him. 'Why are you asking me all these questions, Edward?'

He smiled slightly, then answered her question with another of his own.

'Why do you think?' he said softly.

Of course. He was trying to pick up clues that would lead him to Ria, and he knew that Ria's past and hers were linked. It made sense—but for some crazy reason it depressed the hell out of her.

She put down her coffee-mug. 'It's late, Edward,' she said politely. 'Thank you for the coffee, but now——'

'Don't leave.'

He reached out and put the back of his hand against her cheek. His skin felt hot, as hot as fire, and suddenly she wondered if his body would feel that way the length of hers. And his mouth. Would it be hot, too? Would it brand hers if he kissed her, would it leave a blaze of possession over her breasts, her belly, her thighs...

She rose quickly to her feet. 'I have to,' she said, and he rose, too.

'Olivia.' His voice was thick and urgent. He clasped her face in his hands, threaded his fingers into the silken texture of her hair. 'Stay with me tonight.'

'Don't,' she whispered, but the word was as insubstantial as the flutter of her breath.

'Stay,' he said again. His fingers burrowed into her hair, knotting into its silken texture, holding her captive. 'You know it's what you want to do.'

It was. Oh, God, it was, and that was what made it so awful. She wanted him, this man who thought she was little better than a trollop, she wanted him as she had never wanted anyone.

The sheer perversity of it sent a shudder through her. Had she come unscathed through the awful years of her girlhood only to end up in the arms of a man like Edward Archer? He was cleverer than the others who'd tried to seduce her, that was all, coming at her not with expectations but with soft kisses and whispers.

No. *No*. She wasn't that foolish, no matter what he thought.

She put her hands on his forearms and stepped back. 'You flatter yourself,' she said coldly, 'if you think you know what I want.'

He went very still. A muscle knotted and unknotted in his jaw as he stared down at her.

'Don't do this,' he said, very softly.

'The only thing I'm doing is going home.' She met his gaze. 'Will you call a taxi for me? Or shall I do it myself?'

They stood staring at each other while the seconds ticked away and then Edward's eyes turned as cold as her voice.

'That's not necessary. I'll take you home myself.'

She opened her mouth to argue, but another look at him made her think better of it.

'Thank you,' she said stiffly.

The ride to her town house seemed interminable, even though it was late enough so that the traffic on the usually snarled streets was light. The car seemed even more confining than it had earlier in the day. By the time they pulled into her street, Olivia was ready to burst from her seat.

She started to reach for the door even before Edward had pulled to the kerb, but he reached past her and caught her wrist.

'Wait.' He peered along the kerb, then into the shadows, and she realised he had had the presence of mind to remember what she had forgotten, that anyone might be lurking outside her building, camera or note-pad in hand. 'OK,' he said finally. 'The coast is clear.'

She flung open the door. 'I'm sorry I couldn't help you locate Ria,' she said, the words tumbling out in a rush as she stepped from the car. 'If I think of anything, I'll...'

It was impossible to escape him. He caught her as she hurried towards the safety of the town house, clasped her arm and turned her to face him.

'I'll pick you up at seven tomorrow morning,' he said.

Olivia shook her head. 'What for? I went through all Charles's papers tonight.'

'There are other things to look at. Snapshots, memos.'

'Edward, look, I don't know very much about Ria's relationship with your stepfather. She—she and I aren't very close any more, we haven't been for a long time.'

'How long?'

She looked up, startled at the sudden gruffness in his voice. 'How long is it since you were close?' His hands tightened on her and he drew her into the shadowed doorway. 'Days? Weeks? Months?'

'I don't understand.'

His hands clasped her shoulders. 'When did you stop sharing things?' he whispered roughly. 'Was it before you introduced her to Wright—or after?'

His mouth dropped to hers before she could respond. His question had been harsh but his kiss was gentle, and it was that gentleness that was her undoing. Olivia's palms flattened against his chest; she felt the swift beat of his heart under her fingertips and instead of shoving him from her she made a soft sound and gave in to the sweetness of his mouth.

Edward groaned. His arms swept around her; the tip of his tongue touched the seam of her mouth. Her lips parted and his tongue entered her, stroked and teased until she was dizzy with pleasure. His hands went under her jacket and cupped her buttocks, lifting her against the hardness of his body, then stroking up along her back, her ribs, stopping just beneath her breasts. His thumbs lifted, moved lightly across her nipples, and it was all she could do not to collapse against him.

It was he who ended the kiss, taking her by the shoulders, holding her at arm's length, looking at her while she tried to catch her breath.

He held out his hand. 'Give me your keys,' he said softly.

She wanted to tell him she would do no such thing. I know what you're after, she wanted to say, and I won't let it happen. I won't let you use me, I won't let you reduce me to the woman you think I am.

But he whispered her name softly and kissed her hair, and, trembling, she reached into her purse, took out her keys, and did as he'd commanded. Edward's eyes were hot on her face as he inserted the key in the lock and opened the door.

'Hold out your hand,' he whispered, and when she did, he dropped the keys into her palm and closed her fingers over them. 'Lock up after me,' he said, and then he kissed her one last time, a fierce, hungry kiss she knew would warm her all through the long night ahead.

And then he was gone.

CHAPTER EIGHT

OLIVIA awoke to bright sunshine, a cloudless sky—and the swift, stunning memory of that last moment at her front door. It was as if the intervening hours had rolled back: she could almost feel the brush of Edward's fingers against her skin, hear the rough promise in his voice.

Her heart skipped a beat. What if he had taken the keys from her nerveless fingers, unlocked the door, and stepped into the darkened house with her? Would she have let him lead her up the stairs and into her flat? Would she have let him sweep her into his arms and carry her here, to this bed?

A sigh of despair escaped her lips. What was the point in pretending? She had not spent the night with Edward, but that was less her doing than his.

'Give me your keys,' he had whispered, and she had handed him not just what he'd asked for but the resolve that had kept her safe all these years.

She sat up, tossed aside the blankets, and padded briskly towards the bathroom. All right, it was an embarrassing realisation, but so what? Edward Archer was a very sexy man, and she'd responded to him. Why wouldn't she? she thought as she stepped into the shower. Other women certainly did; she'd seen the way they looked at him that night at Noah's Ark.

What was that old saying? 'Forewarned is forearmed.' Something like that, anyway. And that was what she was now—forewarned. Olivia turned off the shower and reached for an oversized bath sheet. She was human, she was susceptible to him. From now on, she'd be careful. Very careful. Being attracted to a man who thought you had the morals of an alley cat was bad enough, but letting that attraction get the better of you was insane.

The best thing would be to simply not see him again. Olivia peered into the fogged mirror as she towelled her hair dry. And she'd thought about doing exactly that, during the night, but she'd discarded the idea almost as quickly as it occurred.

What counted, more than anything, was locating Ria. And she couldn't do that half as well by herself as she could if she and Edward worked together as a team.

She knew Ria's habits, but he knew Charles's. She knew Ria's likes, but he had access to Charles's papers.

Olivia sighed as she brushed a pale lipstick over her mouth. The simple fact was that she had to go on seeing Edward until they'd located Ria. Once they had, she'd bid him a quick farewell.

And the sooner, the better, she thought as she pulled on grey corduroy trousers and a dusky pink silk shirt. Then her life could get back to normal again. She'd re-open the shop, re-hire Dulcie—and Edward Archer would be nothing but a memory.

Just before seven, Olivia thrust her arms into her anorak and trotted down the stairs. When she came to the door, she reached for the knob without thinking, then snatched her hand back as if it had been burned.

'You have to check first, Olivia,' she whispered through her teeth.

She peered out the window. The commercial centres of Manhattan would be busy at this hour, but her primarily residential street was deserted. Satisfied, she stepped outside.

The sun was angling down into the doorway, filling it with light. Olivia lounged back, eyes closed, face turned up to the warmth, enjoying the serenity of the moment. It seemed a long time since she'd been able to stand peacefully outside her own home.

'You're ready on time. I like that in a woman,' a deep male voice whispered, and her eyes flew open.

'Edward.' She gave a little laugh. 'You startled me.'

He had, but that wasn't really why her heart was pounding. It was seeing him again, and never mind all the things she'd just finished telling herself. It was the way he looked this morning, more handsome than ever in soft blue cords and a cream-coloured fisherman's sweater under an open leather jacket. She thought suddenly of last night, of how they'd stood in this same doorway wrapped in each other's arms, and her face grew hot.

'Taking a chance, aren't you?' he said. 'Standing out here in the open for all the world to see, I mean.'

'Huddling in a doorway isn't exactly standing in the open. Anyway, I checked first.'

'Yeah. I did, too, when I turned the corner.' His shoulders rolled a little under his jacket. 'To tell you the truth, I've just about had it with this nonsense.'

She gave him a little smile. 'Me, too. This morning, I just wanted to yank open the door and step outside, and never mind if a whole army of reporters was waiting!'

Edward grinned. 'A lady with spirit. I like that.'

Why did the simple, teasing words fill her with such warmth?

'Two compliments in less than five minutes,' she said in measured tones. 'I'm overwhelmed.'

His grin widened. 'Don't be too overwhelmed. That's my limit until I've had coffee.'

She couldn't help smiling back. 'In other words, your houseman's still off duty.'

'In other words, I wanted to get an early start. We've a long drive ahead of us.'

'A long drive? What do you mean?'

'I know we said we'd go through more of Charles's papers today——'

'We should go through Ria's too. I thought of that during the night. I couldn't sleep, you see, and——'

'No.' His voice was very soft. 'Nor could I.'

Olivia coloured as their eyes met. 'What I mean is, I thought about our problem, and——'

'So did I.' Edward frowned. 'We've been worrying about this thing the way a dog worries a bone and getting nowhere. Ria's still out there, and we're no closer to her now than we were when we started.'

'I know.'

'If she's gone to ground, I'll bet my life it's someplace where no one would ever connect her with Wright. The last thing she'd want is for some waiter out for a fast buck to put two and two together and call a rag like the *Chatterbox.*'

'I suppose.'

'So what we're going to do today is talk about the Ria you knew years ago, when the two of you were kids.'

'Talk? But I thought——'

He put his arm lightly around her shoulders and drew her out of the doorway. 'Yes. Talk. Who knows what an old memory might dredge up?'

She looked at him doubtfully as he led her towards his car. 'I thought we might stop at the gallery where Ria works,' she said. 'Or pay a visit to Mr and Mrs Bascomb.'

Edward opened the car door and helped her inside. 'My people already checked the gallery.' He came around the car and got in beside her. 'Nobody knows a thing.'

'And Ria's parents? Did they check them, too?'

He gave her a look that said it all. 'I doubt if she's told them anything meaningful in years,' he said softly.

Olivia stared at him for a moment, and then she fell back against the seat.

'You're right,' she admitted.

Edward nodded as he started the engine. 'Today will give us a new perspective,' he said. 'Just you wait and see.'

Where was he taking her? She'd asked, but Edward had refused to answer.

'Where the sharks can't find us,' was all he'd say.

His apartment, she'd thought, but when he'd headed for the Queens Midtown Tunnel she'd realised they weren't going there at all. They weren't going to the park they'd gone to the first time he'd spirited her away, either. It had been north of the city, and the highway he'd just turned on to would take them east.

A long drive, he'd said. Olivia sighed. A long drive in this direction could only lead to one of the posh resort towns that dotted the tip of Long Island. East Hampton, Southampton, Amagansett—one of those picture-postcard places where the rich gathered together in pseudo-English splendour in turreted mini-castles by the sea.

She sighed again. Yes. Edward would own such a summer home, a 'cottage' with umpteen rooms, and why the fact that he did should disappoint her was anybody's guess...

Except that his home wasn't like that at all. The house he drove up to was a handsome, comfortable-looking colonial saltbox nestled in among a stand of tall pine trees. It looked as if it had stood in this spot for centuries.

Edward reached out and shut off the engine. 'Well, here we are,' he said softly. He looked over at her and grinned. 'I warn you, your professional heart is liable to be wounded when you see the interior. The furnishings are mostly hand-me-downs.'

Olivia smiled back at him. 'Why do I get the feeling that they're hand-me-downs other people would call antiques?'

Edward shrugged his shoulders. 'I keep promising myself I'll furnish the place properly, but there's something comfortable about it just as it is, and——'

Something black and large hit the car. Olivia gave a little shriek as a face that seemed to be all sharp white teeth loomed against the window.

'My God,' she gasped, 'what *is* that thing?'

The creature slammed into the car again. It was a dog, an enormous black monster, hurling itself at the door.

Edward's face lit with pleasure. 'Hector,' he said, and in one easy motion he threw open the door and stepped outside.

The monster greeted him by trying to leap into his arms. Olivia watched, a bemused smile curving across her mouth as Edward squatted down and let the huge creature wriggle as much of its front end as it could manage on to his lap. She undid her seatbelt and got out of the car, and Edward looked up at her with a sheepish grin.

'Hector lives up the road,' he said, while the animal panted with joy. 'I've known him since he was just a puppy.'

'Does he always greet you with such exuberance?'

He laughed as he stood up, still stroking the big, square-muzzled head. 'Every time he sees me. It's quite a greeting, isn't it?'

Olivia looked at him. There were muddy paw-prints on Edward's jeans and sweater, his hair was falling into his eyes, and suddenly her heart filled with such a fierce sense of joy that she was afraid she would not be able to speak.

'Yes,' she said softly. 'It is. In fact, I thought he was yours.'

'I wish he were, but I can't see having a dog like that in the city. Someday, maybe, if I move out here permanently...' Hector wagged his tail and edged towards Olivia. 'Don't be afraid of him. He's just a big pussycat.'

She laughed. The dog was pushing his massive head against her leg. 'So I see.' She leaned down a little and petted the animal, but it was clear he was just being polite. Hector's heart belonged to the man beside her.

Edward gave him a loving slap on the rump. 'OK, boy, go on home now. I'll see you again before I leave.' He watched as the dog wandered off into the trees, then held out his hand to Olivia. 'How about the fifty-cent tour?'

He led her up the walk to the porch, warning her to watch for the sagging top step, and then into the house. It was, as she'd thought, at least three hundred years old, dating back to the earliest settlements in the New World. She'd been right, too, about Edward's 'hand-me-downs'. They were beautiful old pieces, hand-worked in pine, oak, and maple, and they suited the house as much as they suited each other.

And as much as they suited Edward. He belonged there, Olivia thought, watching him as he rummaged in the depths of a huge refrigerator. He was like the house, sturdy and strong and weathered, with no artifice or pretension.

'Hey.'

She blinked. Edward was watching her, a little smile on his face.

'Still trying to think of a polite way to tell me that this place could use some work, hmm?'

Olivia shook her head. 'It's a beautiful house,' she said softly.

His smile grew. 'How would you like to have a picnic?'

She laughed. 'On the beach? The weather's lovely, but it's winter in case you hadn't——'

'In the living-room. I'll build a fire in the hearth, we'll spread a blanket and turn on some music.' He grinned as he slammed shut the refrigerator door. 'The only thing missing will be the sand and the ants.'

They feasted on cheese and crackers, wine and crusty bread, finishing it off with fruit and chocolates, and then Edward rolled on to his side, propped his head on his hand, and looked at Olivia. A smile tilted at the corner of his mouth.

'Now,' he said, 'tell me about yourself.'

The warmth that had filled her only seconds before dissipated. She'd almost forgotten why he'd brought her here, but now, with one simple sentence, he'd brought her back to reality.

Tell me about yourself, he'd said, but what he meant was, tell me about Ria.

'There's not much to tell,' she said with a shrug. 'You already know that I met Ria when I was ten and she was eleven. We spent lots of time together then, we were close—really close—until she went off to boarding-school.'

'What about before that?'

'I told you, I didn't know her before——'

'What kind of little girl were you, I mean?' He smiled a little. 'Quiet, and always with your head bent over a book?'

She looked at him. 'How did you know that?'

He shrugged his shoulders. 'Just a good guess.'

She sighed. 'I loved all kinds of stories. Fairy-tales were my special favourite. But Ria——'

'And dolls. I'll bet you liked playing with them, too.'

A slow smile spread across her mouth. 'Oh, yes,' she said softly. 'I did. I had one I called Betty.' She sat up on her knees and stared into the fire. 'Ria didn't much care for dolls.'

'But you were close,' he said quietly.

'Oh, yes. We were inseparable...' She hesitated as she thought back. 'Well, we were at the beginning. But then Ria went away to boarding-school...'

'And you didn't.'

'No, of course not. So I can't even tell you what Ria did when——'

'Why?'

She looked at him. 'Why, what?'

'Why didn't you go to boarding-school, too? Didn't you want to?'

She laughed. 'I'd have loved it. All the kids we knew went. But it was expensive. My aunt couldn't possibly have afforded to send me. That's what I mean when I say I can't help you with Ria. There are lots of things about her that I don't——'

'Were you lonely? You must have been, with only an elderly aunt as companion. What kind of woman was she?'

Olivia thought of Great-Aunt Miriam, who had never quite got over the fact that she had suddenly inherited the responsibility of raising a child nor quite figured out how to do it, and she sighed.

'She was a good woman,' she said simply, 'and she had a kind heart. If she hadn't, I'd have ended up in an orphanage.'

'But she wasn't warm or loving,' Edward said softly.

She shook her head. 'No. Not—not like the mother I lost. Not anything like her.' She fell silent, staring into the flames, and then she cleared her throat. 'You lost your father. I don't have to tell you what it's like.'

'No, I remember how I felt. But I was lucky: I still had my mother, and she was terrific.' He paused. 'Until Charles Wright came along.'

'Was he—was he...I mean, did he always...?' Olivia drew a deep breath. 'It must be awful for your mother, losing him so suddenly, then finding out he'd—he'd...'

She couldn't say any more, not while Edward still believed she'd once been his stepfather's mistress. Olivia's throat constricted. Suddenly, making sure he knew the truth seemed vital.

'Edward,' she said, 'about Charles——'

'None of it was sudden,' he said in clipped tones. 'Wright had a bad heart, and my mother knew it. As for the rest, his cheating, she knew that, too. She just never came right out and admitted it.'

'She knew?'

He got to his feet and stuffed his hands into his pockets. 'I tried to get her to talk about it a couple of times but she wouldn't. So Wright and I played this ugly game of let's pretend—until the day I bumped into you and him at that restaurant.'

'Edward.' Olivia rose to her feet. 'Edward, about that day...'

'I don't want to talk about it,' he said tightly.

'But it's time we did.'

He spun towards her. 'You're going to tell me you weren't one of his women.'

His tone was flat. It was impossible to tell if he'd been expressing scepticism or making a statement. Olivia put her hand lightly on his arm.

'No,' she said, 'I wasn't.'

His eyes locked on her face. She met his gaze squarely, without flinching, and tried to read what he was thinking. It was impossible to tell. The moments ticked away, and then he exhaled.

'The beach is beautiful this time of year,' he said softly. 'Let's take a walk.'

Did he believe her? Was that all there was to setting things straight?

Ask him. Be sure, her head urged. But her heart over-rode the warning. Leave well enough alone, it said. She let him help her into her anorak, take her hand, and lead her out of the back door.

The beach was windswept and empty. Grey boulders rose from the sea and marched across the sand.

'How lovely it is here,' she said softly.

Edward nodded. He slipped his arm around Olivia's shoulders and drew her close into the warmth of his body.

'Yes, it is. It's the most perfect place I know.'

The most perfect place I know. She frowned. Why were those such familiar words?

'It's supposed to be my summer hideaway.' He smiled, and his arm tightened around her. 'But I find myself never closing it down in the autumn, coming here all year long, whenever I can manage.'

'It's wonderful, Edward. The house, the ocean...and those boulders. They're magnificent, like—like a Zen garden planned by giants.'

His hand slid to hers and their fingers laced together. 'Giants with a secret,' he said, tugging her after him.

The secret, she saw with delight moments later, was that at close range the giant rocks revealed a narrow passageway that led to an enclosed world where the wind and the sea were blocked and nothing existed but the blue sky, the hot sun, and the warm white sand—and Edward, standing so close to her that she had only to lift her hand to touch him, Edward, his smile slipping from his face as their eyes met, to be replaced by a look of desire so raw, so potent, that she felt the power of it pierce her soul.

'This is—this is lovely,' she said, trying to defuse the moment.

'Yes,' he said softly, reaching out to her, 'very lovely.'

She shuddered as his fingers trailed across her skin, moving gently along the curve of her cheekbone, tracing the lobe of her ear, the sensitive flesh just below it.

'Edward,' she whispered.

'Do you like it?' he said softly, his hand drifting down her throat. 'When I touch you, I mean.' His voice thickened. 'You do, don't you? Your eyes get dark, like the sky at midnight.' He stepped closer to her. Slowly, his gaze never leaving hers, he eased her jacket from her shoulders. 'And a little pulse throbs to life here,' he said, bending his head and putting his mouth to her throat. 'Olivia,' he whispered. 'Olivia, I want you so badly I ache.'

Her lashes fell to her cheeks. 'We—we said we'd talk,' she said breathlessly. 'But we haven't. Not really. We—we——'

He made a sound that might have been a laugh. 'We have talked.' His fingers were at the buttons to her blouse. They opened slowly, one after another, until the dusky pink silk framed her golden skin and white lace bra. 'But the talking's finished. Now is the time for touching, and kissing, and . . . God, you're so beautiful.' His hand reached out; she moaned as he circled the fullness of one breast with his index finger, moving closer and closer to the already erect centre. 'I want to see your breasts.' His voice thickened, became hoarse. 'I have to see them.' The front clasp of the bra whispered open and he caught his breath. 'Perfect,' he said, 'such perfect breasts.'

'Edward.'

Her voice rose on a little rush of air as he cupped her breasts, his thumbs moving lightly over the crests. Heat shot through her, racing from the flesh beneath his fingertips to a place low in her belly.

'Does your skin taste as sweet as it looks?' he whispered, and he bent his head to her breast and drew a nipple into his mouth.

The touch of his lips banished whatever little bit of sanity she had left. Olivia's head fell back; she reached out and clasped him to her, her fingers tangling fiercely in his hair, while her body strained towards his.

Edward murmured her name as he brought his mouth to hers. His tongue thrust between her lips and she opened to the heat and taste of him. He groaned, his fingers knotting in her hair as he tilted her head back and drew her to him, until she was cradled against the hardness and power of his erection.

'Tell me that you want me,' he whispered, and she gave him her answer, an answer she had never given before, not with words but with every sinuous motion of her body. Her arms went around him, her hands slipping under his sweater to touch the silk of his skin, the firmness of the ridged muscle on his abdomen, the softly abrasive dark hair that curled on his chest. She rose on the balls of her feet and pressed herself more closely into his embrace, and suddenly Edward groaned and swept her up into his arms.

He strode out of their rocky little universe and across the deserted beach while Olivia clung to him, her face buried in his shoulder, her heart beat a pounding counterpoint to the surge of the waves against the shore.

He shouldered the door open, and the sunlit rooms of the house kaleidoscoped around her as he carried her to his bedroom.

He sat down on the edge of the bed and stood her before him, her legs locked tightly between his. Slowly, his eyes never leaving hers, he removed her jacket. When he reached for her blouse, Olivia shook her head.

'I want to see you, too,' she whispered. All the instincts of Eve were hers now; she felt as she had never felt before—seductive, beautiful, sensual beyond her wildest dreams.

Edward's eyes darkened, and then he drew his sweater over his head and tossed it aside. His chest was broad and banded with tight muscle, his shoulders powerful. Dark hair rose in whorls against his tanned skin, tapering to a V that angled below the low-riding waistband of his jeans.

Olivia touched the tip of her tongue to her lips. Tell me that you want me, he had said, and she knew suddenly that she had always wanted him, not just since they'd met but through all the months and years of her life.

I love you, she thought in wonder, I love you, Edward.

When had it happened? When had rage become desire, and desire become love?

'Olivia?' He brought her closer to him. 'I need to hear you say it,' he whispered. 'Tell me you want me. Only me.'

She smiled slowly, determined to answer his question with such joy and passion that he would never need ask it again. He would know, finally, that she had never belonged to any man before.

'Edward,' she said softly, and she smiled slowly and shrugged off her bra and blouse, letting them slip from her shoulders while her eyes held his. 'I want you so much,' she whispered, and she bent towards him, her dark hair falling over her shoulders and breasts, her arms outstretched.

But he didn't clasp her to him. He rose to his feet instead, his mouth twisting until it was a harsh line, his eyes narrowing until they were pinpoints of dark light, and then he spun away from her and stalked to the window. Stunned, Olivia watched his knotted shoulders as he slammed his hands flat against the moulding.

'Edward?' She moved towards him hesitantly. When she was almost beside him, she reached out her hand, then drew it back. 'Edward,' she whispered, 'what is it?'

'Nothing.'

She knew that he was lying. Don't pursue this, she told herself, don't say another word. But the question was already forming on her lips.

'Edward.' She swallowed convulsively. 'Is it—are you thinking of—of...?'

'Of my stepfather?' He swung towards her, and the look on his face sent her stumbling back. 'No,' he said with cold sarcasm, 'of course not. Why would I think of good old Charlie, Olivia? Why would I think about him, at a moment like this?'

A hollow void opened inside her. 'But I told you——'

He pushed past her. 'Get dressed,' he snapped as he grabbed his sweater. 'I'll be waiting outside, in the car.'

She stood staring after him as he stormed from the room and then, with trembling hands, she scooped up her discarded clothing and pulled it on.

'God,' she whispered, 'help me, help me please.'

She turned to the window, looking out at the beach and the beating sea through tear-blurred eyes. The place Edward had called the most beautiful in the world seemed suddenly ugly.

My favourite place, he'd said...

...and then a voice—Ria's voice—whispered through her mind, repeating words scrawled in a childish hand on a postcard, filled with all the wonder a fourteen-year-old child could manage.

'It's just the most beautiful place ever, Livvie,' Ria had written, 'you should see the Bahamas. Oh, it's my favourite, favourite place in the whole world!'

And Olivia knew, with cold clarity, that that was where she would find the friend who had so callously ruined her life.

CHAPTER NINE

'THANK you for calling American Airlines. All of our operators are busy right now, but if you'll please hold on...'

Olivia sighed as the saccharine-sweet recorded voice droned through the telephone line.

'Yes, yes, yes,' she muttered as she tucked the phone into the crook of her shoulder. Of course she'd hold. What else could she do, if she wanted to get to the Bahamas? Although she was beginning to wonder exactly how she was going to manage such a feat. She'd been on the phone most of the morning, calling one airline after another, and she still hadn't come up with a ticket, not even after she'd gritted her teeth and offered to fly first class.

'This is our busiest season, ma'am,' the last operator had said, a touch of condescension tainting the professionally pleasant voice. 'I'm afraid we're sold out through the end of this month—but I can book you through the first week of next. The weather in the Islands is just as pleasant then, and the rate would be a bit lower, too.'

Olivia had almost laughed. What did she care about the weather or the cost? She wasn't arranging a holiday, she was embarking on a journey to the truth. Her trip would end in a confrontation with Ria, one that was sure to write 'finis' to a relationship that had once meant something.

It would not be pleasant but at least it would put an end to the nightmare she'd been living the past weeks. The truth would come out, and then she could go back to leading her own life—without Edward Archer dogging her heels, without him turning her once-placid universe upside-down.

Everything—the days and nights of sneaking past reporters, of being afraid to answer her telephone, of worrying about how long she could hold on to Olivia's Dream before her creditors swooped in for the kill—had come together in one terrible moment, leaving her defenceless, and she'd made an ass of herself in Edward's arms.

The memory was lodged within her like a piece of sharp-edged glass hidden by the sand of a holiday beach, holding the power to cut and wound the unwary. Olivia forced herself to close her mind to it. There was no sense in reliving the embarrassment she'd suffered when she'd offered herself to him. At least she hadn't made a complete fool of herself by giving voice to that pitiful—and absolutely untrue—declaration of love.

She knew now that what she'd felt hadn't been love at all. It had been lust, plain and simple, but her pathetic middle-class morality couldn't deal with something so base. Her conscience had made her substitute one four-letter word for another to make it acceptable. Olivia smiled bitterly. Considering what Edward thought of her, the irony of it was almost beyond belief.

'Thank you for waiting. All of our operators are still busy. If you'll please be patient...'

But none of that mattered any more. She was done playing Edward's game, done clicking her heels at his command. Yes, she would find Ria, but she'd do it on her own—and for her own reasons. She was not naïve enough to think that finding her would solve all her problems. The *Chatterbox*, for example, even when faced with the truth, would never devote equal time to straightening out the mess it had created.

Still, she had to confront Ria and accuse her of treachery, face to face. Ria had thrown her oldest friend into a sea of lies without even asking if she could swim. She'd stolen Olivia's privacy and her reputation, and she might well be the cause of Olivia losing the shop she'd always dreamed of.

And Edward Archer was another one who had used her, he had...

No. Dammit, no! She wouldn't think about him any more. She'd think—she'd think about Ria, instead, about how to find the location of the idyllic place pictured on the dog-eared postcard that lay in her lap, for that was where Ria was hiding. She'd been sure of it ever since yesterday, when she'd suddenly remembered the first Christmas vacation they'd spent apart and the glossy picture postcard Ria had sent her.

She glanced at the photo again, although she'd nearly memorised every palm tree, every pseduo-thatch-roofed hut. 'A View From the Terrace of the Hotel Dorado, the Bahamas', it said in fancy script. Finding the card had been easy enough; it had been just where she'd thought it would be, tucked in among a handful of mementoes in the bottom of the old cigar box that had been her childhood treasure chest.

It was getting to the Bahamas that was turning out to be difficult. She hadn't considered that it would be when she'd made her plans yesterday, during the long taxi ride back to Manhattan. Edward had been determined to drive her home himself, but she'd have walked back to New York rather than sit beside him in that damned little car.

'I brought you here and I'll take you home,' he'd said curtly, despite her demand that he let her phone for a taxi. 'Now, get in the car!'

There'd been no sense arguing with him. One look at his shuttered, arrogant face had told her that much. It was so typical, she'd thought furiously, men like him went through life getting their own way.

Well, that was over as far as she was concerned. He just didn't know it yet.

Olivia had climbed into his car as ordered. When they'd reached the village, she'd turned to him.

'Is there a pharmacy?' she'd asked in a coldly polite voice.

Edward hadn't even glanced at her. 'Why?'

'I have a headache, and I want to buy some aspirin. Does that meet with your approval?'

His jaw had tightened, but he'd said nothing, he'd only pulled sharply to the kerb.

'I'll get it for you.'

But Olivia had already opened her door and slipped out on to the pavement.

'I'll do it myself,' she'd said, and after that it had been easy. She'd hurried into the front door of the pharmacy and yes, thank heavens, there was a rear exit! It led to a service alley which opened on to a veritable rabbit warren of narrow streets. She'd trotted up one and down another, until finally she'd spotted a public telephone booth where she'd called for a taxi. The trip home had cost a bloody fortune—she'd had to ask the driver to wait while she withdrew cash from the automatic bank machine on the corner to pay her fare—but it had been worth it, not just because she hadn't had to sit trapped in the car with Edward but because she'd had the pleasure of imagining how infuriated he must have been when he realised she'd slipped away...

'American Airlines, Carol speaking. How may I help you?'

Olivia wasted no time on polite preliminaries. 'When is your first flight to the Bahamas?'

'I'm sorry, ma'am. I have nothing available until late next——'

'This is an emergency. You must have something.'

'Let me see...' The line filled with clicks and whirrs. 'I do see a cancellation, ma'am.'

'Wonderful!'

'The flight leaves in an hour and a half.'

Olivia's gaze flew to her watch. 'That's not a problem,' she said with more conviction than she felt. But it wouldn't be, if she didn't pack, if she could get a cab, if there were no traffic...

'It's first class,' the clerk said, quoting a price that made Olivia blanch. But she didn't hesitate.

'I'll take it.'

She put the charges on her credit card, and hotel charges, too, later that night at Nassau International Airport after a clerk at the tourist information desk managed to find her what might well have been the last available room on the island. She began a mental tally of all the charges she'd incurred as she taxied to her hotel, but the numbers were dizzying and finally she gave up. There were more things to buy tomorrow—clothes to get through the next few days—but who cared what this was costing? When the bill arrived, she'd be bankrupt anyway.

All that counted now was finding Ria.

Olivia had a plan—a simple one, but what more did she need? After all, she had a photo, and the name of a hotel. It was like looking up and finding an arrow drawn across the sky, leading to Ria.

The first chink in the plan appeared the next morning, while she was drinking her coffee and leafing through a tourist brochure in the hotel dining-room.

One sentence fairly leaped off the page.

'Seven hundred islands make up the Bahamian chain.'

She stared at the words in disbelief. 'Seven hundred?' she asked in horrified tones of the waiter serving her breakfast.

The man grinned. 'And all very beautiful, miss,' he said in the beautiful, singsong tones of the islands.

They were not, it turned out, all inhabited. But that was nothing to get excited about, since almost two dozen supported some of tourist facilities. Two dozen, she thought with a muffled groan. Two dozen!

It was a good thing she had a photo, and a hotel name, she thought as she opened the telephone directory and began leafing through it.

'Hotel Dorado,' she mumbled, 'Hotel Dor...'

There was no Hotel Dorado. Not on New Providence Island. And not on Grand Bahama, nor on Eleuthera. There was one on Great Abaco, and she spent an entire day and an incredible amount of money travelling there. But the Hotel Dorado she found looked nothing like the one on the postcard, and when she asked the manager if the hotel had been redone, he smiled and assured her that it had not existed at all until two years before.

By the day's end, she felt footsore and defeated. How stupid she'd been, to have assumed that the hotel pictured on the card would still exist. Even if it did, there was no guarantee it had the same name. The card was years old and besides, commercial establishments came and went. On the street where Interiors by Pierre was located, there was a little shop that had gone through three owners and four names in less than two years.

She was depressed and upset when she boarded the boat for New Providence. She stood off by herself, resting her arms on the railing and staring blankly out to sea.

'Excuse me, miss, but are you all right?'

She started at the sound of the pleasant male voice. When she looked up, her face went white. Edward, she thought, and her heart turned over.

But, of course, it wasn't Edward, it was only a man with dark hair and dark eyes, and after she could speak, she said she was fine, thank you, and she turned blindly to the sea again.

She slept badly that night, tossing and turning until the sheets were a tangled mess. She dreamed, too, endless dreams about Edward, none of them very clear or even comprehensible. But she awoke from each with her lashes damp and a hollow feeling in her breast.

It was hatred, that was what it was. She hated Edward, she was consumed with hatred for him. She lay in the bed and stared into the dark while she thought of what she should have said to him in that East Hampton bedroom, thinking of the things she *would* say to him, if she were ever unfortunate enough to see him again. Eventually, she dozed off. If she dreamed, she had no memory of it. But when she awoke, her eyes were swollen and that nameless emptiness was in her heart again.

It had to be Ria she dreamed of, Ria and the way she'd betrayed their friendship.

What else could possibly fill her with such terrible sorrow?

The days slipped away, as did her memory. She moved from the hotel to a tiny guest house, counted up her last dollars, and decided to try and better the odds.

She chose an investigator from an ad in the phone book and paid him a visit.

'I need to locate this place,' she said, handing him the yellowing postcard.

'How old is this thing?' he asked as he fingered it.

'Ten years.'

The man nodded. 'Any idea which island the place is on?'

Olivia shook her head. 'None.'

He nodded again and tipped back his chair. 'Well, I can do some checking. There'll be old files, papers, surveys...' He looked up and shrugged. 'Maybe we'll turn something up.'

'And if we don't?'

He shrugged again. 'I can hire a helicopter, maybe a plane, do some aerial photography. Depends on how badly you want to find the place and how much you got to spend.' He grinned as he shoved the card across the desk. 'Hubby took off, you figure he went to ground here?'

'No. It's nothing like that.'

'Must be pretty important, though, huh?'

'What would it cost? For the things you just mentioned?'

He tapped his finger against his lip, then named a sum that made her collapse back into her chair.

'It's up to you to decide,' he said. 'This kind of thing's never cheap. Is finding this place worth it to you or not?'

At sunset, sitting in the quiet cove behind the guest house, her back pressed against the rough bark of a coconut palm, she thought of what he'd asked her. Not that there was any question of hiring the man: the cost of his services was out of the question.

But his queries had unsettled her. *Was* finding Ria worth all this? The money. The time. The anguish. Olivia scooped up a handful of sand and let it flow through her fingers. The story about her and Wright was old news. Given another week or two, would anybody really remember it? New Yorkers, especially, were served gossip with their breakfast toast. Would any of them even be able to link her name with Wright's in another few months?

She scooped up another handful of the fine white grains and watched as they drifted away. Maybe she'd be better off going home and spending the last of her dollars on Olivia's Dream. She could phone Dulcie, tell her it was time to start work again. She could take out an ad, a discreet one, announcing that the studio was reopening after a brief hiatus. Hadn't some Fifth Avenue shop on the verge of bankruptcy done that once, cool as you please, as if they'd only been closed briefly for their own pleasure? Or she could change the name, as so many others had done.

Olivia closed her eyes wearily. Why had she come here in the first place? To confront Ria, yes, but to what end?

'Ria,' she'd say, 'you betrayed our friendship.'

But Ria knew that, for God's sake! What would it really serve to tell her so? As for getting her to make a statement to the *Chatterbox*—Olivia sighed. It was a great idea, but Ria would never agree to do it. In her heart, she'd known that all the time.

Why, then, had she come? Her reasons seemed as insubstantial as smoke.

She drew her legs up, sat forward, and locked her arms around her knees while she stared out at the sea. There was a boat out on the water; in the deepening blue of twilight, it almost seemed to be sailing not on the sea but across the sky.

Olivia sighed. Life could be like that. You'd look at one thing but see another. It was how Edward saw her, the way he'd always see her, unless she found Ria and made her tell the truth, that it was she and not Olivia who'd been his stepfather's mistress.

Her heart fluttered. Was that why she'd come here? Because she wanted to give Edward proof of her innocence?

She rose and began walking slowly along the shore, the water lapping and foaming across her bare feet. No. It wasn't possible. She hated Edward. She despised him. She never wanted to see him again. If by some twist of fate he turned up this very moment, she'd—she'd turn on him in fury, she'd slap his face, she'd tell him he was the cruellest, most insensitive bastard the world had ever known.

Her throat constricted. But he wouldn't. He wouldn't come after her, he wasn't thinking of her, dreaming of her, he wasn't . . .

'Olivia.'

The voice that had called out her name was soft as the breeze that carried it, but it sent her stumbling to a sudden halt. Her heartbeat stuttered, accelerated, then began to race within her breast.

It couldn't be Edward. It was only her imagination working overtime. She took a deep, deep breath and then she turned slowly, her hand to her heart as if to hold it still. The sun was lying on the breast of the sea, blazing defiantly at the encroaching darkness, and the man calling her was bathed in the molten gold light, looking like a god come down from Olympus.

It was Edward.

They stood staring at each other while the sun melted into the sea. The fury she'd felt only moments ago fled and in its place was dizzying exhilaration. He had come after her!

A chill went through her. Was she crazy? Of course he had come. He had come for what he'd wanted all along, Ria and the Gemini stock.

Olivia waited as he walked towards her, her posture stiff and unyielding despite the thready race of her heart. When she spoke, her voice was cold.

'How did you find me?'

'You really didn't think you could hide from me, did you?'

His voice was low, taut with control, and she realised suddenly that all of him was like that, held in check, as if he were afraid he might, at any moment, shatter. Anger, she thought, anger and rage were driving him, the same as they drove her. That *was* what she felt— wasn't it?

'Me, hide from you?' She managed a smile. 'What an imagination you have, Edward.'

His mouth twisted. 'I suppose you'd like me to think you came here on vacation.'

'I don't much care what you think,' she said, and she started past him. But she'd only taken a couple of steps when he reached out and caught her wrist.

'You took a hell of a chance, Olivia.' His voice was a low growl. 'Running away from me that night...'

'You should have listened when I said I wanted to go back to the city by myself.'

He gave a short, barking laugh. 'I should have listened to a lot of things.'

'This is all pointless. You wasted your time coming here.'

His hand tightened on her. 'What makes you so sure?'

'You won't find what you came for.'

He stepped closer to her, so close that she had to tilt her head back to see his face. Was that why she felt suddenly light-headed, because of the odd angle at which she stood?

'Won't I?' he said softly.

'No. I'm not going to help you find Ria. I don't want anything more to do with this. Or with you.'

'I haven't asked you to help me.'

'No. But you will. I'm just saving us the——'

'My people turned the city upside-down,' he said gruffly. His hand moved against her skin, slipping to her shoulder, clasping it and turning her to him so that they were standing breath to breath. 'That's where I thought you were, at first, in New York, hiding from me.'

'Stop using that word. Why would I——?'

'But you weren't.' He lifted her hand between them and clasped it against his chest. She could feel the rapid thud of his heart beating against her palm. 'No one had seen you, not your attorney, not that little girl who works for you...'

'Dulcie? You involved Dulcie in this?' Olivia twisted against his hand. 'You shouldn't have done that. She doesn't know anything about Ria.'

'I don't want to talk about Ria, dammit! Don't you understand that yet?'

His voice was harsh and angry, but the touch of his hand moving lightly along her cheek, smoothing her wind-tossed hair back from her face, was soft and gentle. Suddenly they seemed to be standing on another beach, more than a thousand miles to the north, with only the sky and the ocean to see them.

Olivia caught her breath as Edward took her face in his hands and urged it up to his.

'Look at me,' he whispered, and slowly, very slowly, her lashes lifted and her eyes met his. 'Do you know what the hell you put me through?'

She wanted to make a flippant response, to tell him that if he was expecting an apology he'd have a long wait.

But how could she, when he was looking at her this way, when his thumbs were stroking lightly across her skin?

'I couldn't imagine what had happened to you, whether you were alive or dead.' He shook his head. 'I kept thinking, hell, she's such a stubborn woman——'

'I'm not,' she said, standing stiffly within his embrace.

Edward laughed softly. 'And independent. Too damned independent for your own good.' He rested his forehead against hers. 'It was almost a relief when my people finally found out you'd gone to the islands.'

'You had no right to check up on me,' Olivia said. She meant to sound angry, or at least accusatory, but she couldn't seem to manage it. There was a little tremor in her voice, one that matched the tremor in her body. Her muscles felt as if they were softening, as if they weren't going to be able to hold her up very much longer.

'Let go of me, Edward. I—I don't feel——'

She caught her breath as he put his arms around her and gathered her to him.

'I know how you feel,' he whispered. 'You feel like—like a summer sunset, everything warm and beautiful, with the smell of lilacs in your hair.'

God. Oh, God, why was she letting him do this to her? It was all happening again, just as it had the last time they'd been together. He was touching her, kissing her, whispering soft little words in her ear as he brushed back her hair, pressing his lips to her skin—and it would end as it had before, in an icy hail of accusation and rage.

And she would not survive it. Not this time. Olivia felt the swift rise of tears in her eyes. Had she come all this distance only to end up in his arms again, when they both knew she didn't belong there?

'Edward——'

'What, sweetheart?'

His voice was soft, as soft as the breeze that blew across the sand, bearing the scent of the tropical night.

'Edward,' she said, 'I beg you...' She cried out as he undid the first few buttons of her dress and slid his hands inside. 'Don't—don't do this. Don't...' She moaned as his fingers moved across her breasts. 'Edward, I don't want—I don't...'

'My love,' he whispered.

Her head fell back as he bent and kissed her, his mouth hot and open over hers, his hands cupping her breasts. She cried out as their bodies met, and she knew she could no longer resist what she so desperately wanted. Her arms went around him, looping tightly around his neck, and he made a sound in the back of his throat and drew her closer, kissing her and kissing her until she was dizzy with need, aching with desire.

'I can't wait,' he whispered.

His hands slid to her waist and he lifted her skirt, bunching the fabric in the small of her back. His thumbs hooked in her panties and he slid them down her legs. Kneeling before her, he curved his hand around her ankle, lifted her foot, and discarded the wisp of silk that was tangled at her feet.

Edward leaned forward and buried his face against her cotton skirt, pressing his mouth to her until she could feel the heat of his kiss through her clothing. His hands were on her skin, cool against her heated flesh, touching her where she'd never been touched. When she felt the first, faint brush of his fingers against her thighs, she cried out.

They dropped to the sand together, wrapped in each other's arms, sharing sweet, hungry kisses. Edward eased her dress from her shoulders; she felt the warmth of his breath on her skin and then the scalding heat of his mouth. Her arms tightened around him and she lifted herself towards him.

She had told herself what she felt for him was only sexual desire, but that had been a lie. Desire could make your head pound and your blood race, but it couldn't make your heart swell in your breast until it felt as if it would explode. It couldn't make you feel this fierce need to match kiss for kiss, touch for touch; it couldn't make tears rise and tremble on your lashes.

There was only one emotion that could do that, the one she'd refused to acknowledge. With a little sigh, she let the words she'd tried so hard to deny slip from her lips.

'I love you,' she said, 'oh, Edward, I...'

Her broken whisper trembled and died as he went still in her arms. It was too late to call the foolish words back; she waited for him to put her from him, to laugh and turn her pitiable confession into the worst kind of joke.

But he did none of that. Instead, he took her face in his hands and kissed her deeply, and then he rose and drew her up beside him. Slowly, his eyes never leaving her face, he closed the buttons of her dress and then he kissed her again.

'Come with me,' he said softly.

He led her across the sand to where his car waited, swung the door open and helped her in, giving her one long, final kiss before he went around to slip behind the wheel. The engine roared to life and suddenly she remembered.

She was naked under her skirt.

Heat coursed through her blood, and she whispered Edward's name.

He looked over at her. In the shadowed darkness, his face was mysterious, hard with sensuality.

'Yes?'

She touched the tip of her tongue to her lips. 'My — my panties...'

His hand slipped under her skirt, stopping just before it reached her thighs.

'You won't need them.'

'But—but I can't just—I can't...'

He leaned across the console and caught her hair in his fist, tilting her head back, and then he kissed her deeply.

'I won't touch you,' he said in a fierce whisper. 'Not while we're in the car. Do you understand, Olivia? I want to think about you and I want you to think about me, and what it's going to be like when we finally make love.'

Her throat went dry. She wanted to answer, to tell him that what was happening was beyond anything she had ever dreamed, let alone experienced, but it was too late. His foot came down hard on the accelerator and, with a spray of gravel, the car shot forward into the night.

CHAPTER TEN

HIS car was almost a duplicate of the one he drove in New York, long and low and built for speed. Only days before, Olivia had abhorred the sense of enforced intimacy it demanded. Now, as they hurtled through the black night under clouds that stampeded across the moon, their closeness only heightened the excitement pulsing through her blood.

Edward took her hand and held it tightly against his thigh, never letting it go, so that when he shifted gears she performed the action with him. It was only a single point of contact, yet she felt as if their bodies were already coming together. She swayed against him as they rounded a curve and she caught his scent, cleanly masculine and powerful.

'Edward,' she whispered, just that, his name and nothing more, because she knew that what they needed to say to each other could best be said in each other's arms, and she knew he understood because he lifted her hand to his mouth and kissed her palm.

She had no idea how long it took before they reached his villa. She was beyond reason and thought, caught up in a passion so great that it had narrowed her world to this man and this moment.

He pulled the car to a stop outside an isolated house on a curving beach. Edward lifted her into his arms and took her lips in a fierce and hungry kiss.

She clung to him as he carried her through the darkness, up and up into a room filled with the scent of the sea and the milky wash of moonlight. Her hands were on his shoulders when he lowered her to her feet, her breath catching as he brought her slowly down the length of his body, and she was seared by the heat and

145

hardness of him. Her breasts brushed against his chest, the sensitive nipples tightening at the feel of him against her, and when she felt the heat of his arousal press into her loins she moaned his name.

'Yes,' he whispered, his voice rough, almost alien. 'Yes,' and his fingers went to the buttons at her collar, opening them, one by one. His eyes were pools of darkness, his nostrils flared with desire, and she trembled as she realised the effort it was costing him not to rip the dress from her with one sweep of his hand.

When the buttons were undone to her waist, he framed her face in his hands.

'Olivia,' he said, and she thought her name had never sounded so sweet, so beautiful.

He bent and put his mouth to hers, kissing her gently, teasingly, giving her nibbling little kisses until her lips parted and she arched towards him, asking for more without saying a word. She returned his kisses, the tip of her tongue tracing the outline of his mouth, and he growled something as he gathered her close. His open mouth slanted across hers.

When he put her from him, she was dizzy. She swayed, and he caught her by the waist.

'Edward,' she murmured.

'Yes, love.'

Her sigh whispered into the night. 'Don't stop. Please.'

He slipped her dress from her shoulders and let it fall to her hips, then opened the front clasp of her bra and drew that away, too. Her lashes lifted from her cheeks as he stepped back a little, and she watched as his eyes moved slowly over her face, her throat, her naked breasts.

'How beautiful you are,' he whispered.

Colour rose in her cheeks. 'Don't—don't look at me like that,' she said. 'It—it embarrasses me.'

His gaze lifted to hers. She saw something glint in the darkness of his eyes, surprise, perhaps, or a more complex emotion, and he caught her wrists as she lifted her hands to shield herself.

'Don't stop me,' he said fiercely. 'I want to see you.'

She stood, trembling, as he undressed her, until at last she was naked before him. She felt completely at his mercy as his eyes swept over her. She could feel her blood throb wildly everywhere he looked, staining her skin crimson, exposing her vulnerability to him. His gaze dropped to her breasts and she felt them lift, felt the centres tighten.

Edward groaned and caught her in his arms.

'Do you know how it excites me to see that you want me?' he whispered. He swept aside her hair, exposing her neck, and pressed his open mouth to her flushed skin. 'I've waited so long, Olivia, I've wanted you for so long.'

For a lifetime, she thought, as long as I've waited for you. She had never imagined she could feel this way in any man's arms, engulfed in the white-hot fire of sensation and in the silken feel of his skin, with time delineated only by sensation.

His fingers moved on her flesh, and Olivia moaned as he cupped her breasts in his hands, then lowered his head and drew her nipple into the heat of his mouth. She cried out at the electric contact and her arms tightened around him, her fingers burrowing into the silk of his hair as she clasped his head to her.

'My beautiful, beautiful darling,' he murmured, and the endearment that had once been a cruel insult now filled her heart with hope. His hands slipped to her waist and then he dropped to his knees before her, holding her, lifting her to him. He pressed his mouth to her, trailing kisses across her belly, and suddenly his mouth was on her.

Olivia's head fell back and she cried out, in shock and in passion.

'No. You mustn't! Edward...'

Her breathless plea faded as he stroked and kissed her, and finally with a cry of surrender, she gave herself up to him, slipping beyond reality, moaning softly under the slide of his tongue and the heat of his hands. She was all the colours of the rainbow, a rainbow that arced higher and higher until suddenly it shattered into a million fiery pieces and she collapsed against him.

'Edward,' she cried, and he rose, lifted her spent body in his arms and carried her to the bed with swift, impatient strides. She fell back against the silken softness of satin sheets and feather pillows, watching through half-closed eyes as he stripped away his clothing until he stood revealed before her, all hard muscle and golden skin in the ivory moonlight. How beautiful he was, how proud in his maleness.

'Olivia,' he whispered, and when their eyes met, she knew she could no more have denied this night than she could have stopped the high-riding clouds from racing across the sky.

Smiling, she raised her arms to him.

'Come to me,' she said.

And he did.

Later, Olivia lay close in the curve of Edward's arm, her head cradled against his shoulder. The moon had slipped from the sky, plunging the room into darkness. Edward stroked the damp, tangled curls back from her cheeks while he nuzzled gentle kisses into her hair.

'Why didn't you tell me?' he whispered.

She closed her eyes, remembering the instant when he had made her his, the deep, piercing thrust that had frozen him into immobility.

'Olivia!' His voice had become hoarse. 'God! I never dreamed ...'

She'd reached up and brought his head down to hers, silencing his questions with her mouth, urging him on with the movement of her hips, until finally he'd groaned and buried himself deeply in her. Now, in the sweet afterglow of lovemaking, his voice still reflected his shock.

'You should have told me,' he said softly.

'That I was a virgin?' She gave a sad little laugh. 'That's not something you announce to a man, Edward—not even to convince him that you haven't slept with his stepfather.'

'Hell! When I think of the things I said to you——'

Olivia shook her head. 'Forget all that,' she said softly.

His arm tightened around her. 'How can you ever forgive me? I've done things to you that—that——'

'None of that matters now.' She sighed as she kissed his throat. 'It's all behind us.'

'But it isn't,' he said. She could feel the sudden tensing of his muscles. 'I have to explain——'

'No,' she whispered, 'you don't.' She rose up on her elbow, her hair tumbling across her bare shoulder. 'I'm not blameless either. I could have—should have—insisted you listen to the truth from the start, but you never gave me the chance, and then, after a while, I was so angry that I let you think whatever you liked.'

His hand curled around the nape of her neck and he brought her head to his chest.

'Ria,' he said through his teeth, 'that damned Ria! Everything that's happened is her fault. God, I'd like to strangle that bitch!'

Olivia put her finger across his lips. 'Remember what you said? That you didn't want to talk about her? That's how I feel, too. I don't even want to hear her name.'

Edward blew out his breath. 'I understand, darling. But——'

'You did mean it, didn't you? That Ria wasn't important?'

'Olivia——' Time seemed to stand still, and then Edward sighed, drew her into his arms, and kissed her. 'Nothing is important except this,' he whispered. After a long, long time, he lay back against the pillows, still holding her close. 'I can't believe no man's ever claimed you,' he said softly.

Olivia punched her shoulder lightly. 'You're such a male chauvinist,' she said, and smiled. 'Would it ever occur to you that I had something to do with that?'

He grinned. 'You did, huh?'

She nodded. 'Don't let it go to your head, but I was waiting for the right man to come along.'

Edward kissed her. 'Thank you for waiting,' he whispered.

'You're welcome,' she said with teasing solemnity, and then she cleared her throat. 'I was all right, then? Not—not a disappointment?'

'A disappointment?'

'You know what I mean.'

He laughed and kissed her nose. 'If it's compliments you want——'

'Well, you'd thought I was some sort of—of courtesan,' she said quickly, 'and then I turned out to be——'

'You turned out to be wonderful,' he said softly. He brushed his mouth against hers. 'In fact, you're everything I'd ever dreamed of.'

Olivia sighed and kissed his chest. 'Really?'

He laughed and tugged at her hair. 'You *are* fishing for compliments, woman.' His fingers knotted gently in her hair and he drew her head back. 'And I've got one for you.'

She smiled again. 'What?'

'This.'

His hand moved on her, and she gave a little gasp. 'Edward! What are you doing?'

'What does it feel as if I'm doing?' he growled.

'But—but can you? So soon, I mean . . .'

He took her hand in his and brought it to him, closing her fingers around his maleness.

'What do you think, darling?' he said in a husky whisper. 'Is it too soon?'

And then he parted her thighs and thrust into her, and the world spun away.

Olivia awoke slowly, stretching languorously in soft golden sunshine.

'Edward,' she whispered, reaching out for him—but he was gone.

Her heart skipped a beat. She sat up, clutching the blanket to her breasts, just as the door swung open.

'Good morning.'

There he was, smiling at her from the doorway. He was wearing nothing but a very brief pair of white cotton shorts, and the sight of his lean, muscled body brought back memories of the long, sweet night. It was stupid to feel shy, after all they'd shared, but she couldn't help it. A flush rose in her cheeks.

'Good morning,' she said, clutching the blankets tighter.

Edward's smile tilted as he came towards her. 'I was getting desperate out there,' he said. 'I've peeked in on you every ten minutes for the last hour——'

'The last hour? You mean, you've been up all that time while I——'

'And each time I did, you were lying on your back with your arms flung out, sprawled across the bed...'

'Me? Me, lying with my arms flung out?'

'...looking as if you were going to snore the day away while I faced starvation in the kitchen.'

Olivia's chin lifted. 'Wrong on all counts. I do not sleep sprawled. I do not snore. And if you're going to tell me that you were waiting for me to make you breakfast...'

Edward dropped to the bed beside her. 'OK,' he said, 'I'm guilty on all counts. You sleep in the curve of my arm, as if you were made to fit against me. The only sounds you make are those soft little moans when I touch you. And——'

'Never,' she said, although it was hard to put much vehemence into the word when he was so close. 'I never make any sounds at all when I sleep.'

He bent and kissed her mouth. 'And the only reason I was out there starving,' he whispered, 'is because I didn't want to make our breakfast until I was sure you were awake.'

Olivia smiled. 'You're making breakfast?'

'Don't sound so shocked. Yeah, I'm making breakfast. Fresh orange juice, bacon and eggs, biscuits...'

Her eyes widened. 'Biscuits?'

'Well, they came in a box, but they have to be put in the oven before you can eat 'em.' He grinned. 'Impressed?'

Suddenly, all her shyness was gone, replaced by a feeling of love so intense that it made her throat constrict. She reached up and clasped his face between her hands.

'I'm afraid you'll have to try a lot harder to impress me, Mr Archer.'

His smile faded. 'You're a hard woman to please,' he said huskily. The blanket fell away as he reached for her. 'I guess I'm just going to have to try something else.'

'I don't know if anything will work. I mean, you'll have to come up with something really clever...'

He laughed wickedly. 'Like this?'

Her breath caught. 'Oh. Oh, yes. Like that. Like...'

Passion swallowed them up.

By the time they got to it, breakfast was really a late brunch. And it was not, Edward kept saying, his best effort. The bacon was burned at the edges and the biscuits charred all over; the eggs were the consistency of soft shoe leather. But then, that was bound to happen when two people kept stopping what they were doing to share coffee-flavoured kisses in the sunlit kitchen.

They ate at a little glass-topped table on a terrace overlooking the sea, alone except for a tiny lizard with emerald eyes that clung to the railing like a jewelled statue. Beyond, white sand stretched to the turquoise sea.

'How beautiful it is,' Olivia said softly.

Edward smiled at her. 'You're what's beautiful.'

She smiled back at him. 'You're not half bad looking yourself.'

He grinned, then gave his attention to his breakfast. Olivia's smile faded as she watched him. Her words had been said lightly, but she'd spoken the truth. Seated opposite her, his dark hair still damp from the shower they'd shared, with the sun beating down on his naked shoulders and muscled arms, Edward was every woman's dream.

'None of that,' he'd said sternly when she'd started to collect last night's discarded clothing from the floor. 'We dress formally for breakfast.'

Which meant, Olivia thought with a little laugh, that now she wore a stretched-out T-shirt bearing a faded Harvard logo while Edward wore a pair of shorts that left most of his beautiful body uncovered.

And he *was* beautiful, not just in how he looked but in all the ways that counted. Prepared to dislike him, she'd twisted everything that he was, mistaking self-assurance for arrogance, strength for dominance, determination for insolence.

Her old enemy had suddenly taken a face and a name and become the man she loved.

If only she could tell him that, she thought, not in the throes of passion but now, with the early afternoon light shining down, with a table between them and all the everyday things of life surrounding them. If only she could say, I love you, Edward, as easily as she might say, would you please pass the sugar?

But she had said it once, and he had not answered . . .

'. . . for your thoughts.'

Olivia blinked. Edward was leaning towards her, a ghost of a smile on his lips.

'I—I'm sorry,' she said. 'I must have been day-dreaming. Did you say something?'

'I offered the proverbial penny for your thoughts.' His smile widened as he took her hand and brought it to his mouth. 'Unless you'd rather have a kiss...?'

She looked at him helplessly. 'They weren't—they weren't worth a penny.'

His eyebrows drew together in a mocking frown. 'Are you saying my kisses aren't worth a penny?'

'No. No, of course not. I just——'

'Hey.' His voice went soft; he pressed a kiss into the palm of her hand, then closed her fingers over it. 'I was only teasing you, sweetheart.'

Olivia blew out her breath. 'Sorry.' She gave him a tremulous smile. 'I think—I think all this fresh air and sunshine must have frazzled my brain. I've been in these islands for days, but I never...'

'Never what?'

She shrugged her shoulders. 'I know it sounds ridiculous, but I never really saw them. I—I was just so busy concentrating on other things...'

His hand tightened on hers. 'From now on, just concentrate on me,' he said, almost fiercely.

She waited for him to say something more, but he didn't. After a minute, she cleared her throat. 'Edward? How did you find me?'

He put down his coffee. 'You left a plastic trail a mile wide, darling.'

'A what?'

'Each time you charged a purchase to your credit card, they dutifully recorded the time and place.'

'Of course.' She hesitated. 'And you figured I'd come here looking for Ria?'

He reached out and stroked her cheek. 'Well, I didn't think you'd suddenly decided on a mid-winter vacation.'

'No,' she said with a little smile, 'no, I—I...' She cleared her throat. There was another question that had to be asked, a stupid one, considering that she knew the answer, but . . .

'Edward?' She swallowed. 'Did you come to the islands looking for me? Or—or for Ria?'

His eyes darkened. 'Last night, you said you were done helping me search for her.'

She had, but that was before they'd become lovers. What she'd wanted then was to put an end to everything that connected them, to put Edward out of her life once and for all. And the simplest way to do it, she'd been certain, was to refuse to be party to his quest for Ria Bascomb.

But that had all changed now. She loved Edward with all her heart, and if she wasn't quite foolish enough to think he'd fallen in love with her, too, she knew that he felt something for her, something that might even transcend the undeniable passion she roused in him.

And, if she loved him, was it right to deny him what he wanted? He had endless resources at his command. All she had to do was give him the postcard lying back in her hotel room, and his search would be ended.

'Olivia?' She looked up. 'Isn't that what you said?'

She touched her tongue to her lips. 'Well, yes. But——'

'No "buts",' he said firmly. He leaned forward and kissed her. 'End of discussion.'

'But what about the stock Charles left her? You were so determined to get it back . . . Are you saying you're just going to forget about it?'

He shook his head. 'End of discussion, I said.' He clasped her hands in his and drew her to her feet. 'Now, come on. We've things to do today.'

She smiled. 'We have?'

'Uh huh. For starters, we've got to drive to that place you were living in and get your things packed.'

'Ah.' She sighed as she burrowed into his arms. 'I almost forgot. We have to go back to New York.'

Edward's hands slid gently up and down her spine. 'No, we don't.'

'We don't?' Olivia leaned back in his arms. 'But I thought—I mean, now that you've given up on finding Ria...'

'Why would we want to go back to cold, grey winter when we can stay here, in the warm sunshine?'

'We?'

'Yes. I thought we'd move your things in here and stay for a while. How's that sound?'

'Stay here, you mean? Together?'

Edward smiled a little. 'Well, with the lizard for company, of course.' He kissed her gently. 'OK?'

Olivia stared at him. He wanted her to move in here, to stay with him. Why did that seem so very different from simply spending the night?

'If you're thinking about reopening Olivia's Dream...'

She wasn't. She hadn't even thought of Olivia's Dream, not since Edward had first taken her in his arms last night.

'...you must know it's too soon,' he said softly. 'People will forget, in time, but——'

'But that time isn't quite yet.' She nodded. 'I know. But moving in here, with you...'

'And the lizard. Don't forget the lizard.' When she didn't answer, his smile dimmed a little. 'Too much sea, sand, and solitude, hmm? Well, we can check into a hotel, then. I know one on Eleuthera that——'

'Oh, no,' she said quickly. 'It isn't that.' Her cheeks turned pale pink. 'I mean, the thought of—of being alone here with you is—is...' Her courage failed her. 'It's very nice,' she finished lamely.

'Very nice?' Edward began to laugh. 'Very nice?' He turned to the lizard. 'Did you hear that, pal? Here I cooked this spectacular breakfast for this woman——'

'Edward——'

'I spent the night making mad, passionate love to her——'

'Edward,' she said again, trying not to smile, 'listen——'

'What's that, pal?' He frowned. 'The lizard says you couldn't possibly have any complaint about my lovemaking.'

Olivia laughed softly. 'Is that right?'

'He says it's the thought of living on burned bacon and overcooked eggs that has you worried.'

'Edward, honestly——'

'So he wants me to point out that there's a house-keeper comes in every day to do the cleaning and the cooking.' He gathered her close to him, and his voice fell to a whisper. 'Don't you want to stay here with me, darling?'

She hesitated. Of course, she did. But it wasn't right, her dreary, middle-class self was whispering, moving in with a man just wasn't right.

Olivia leaned her head against Edward's shoulder. Wasn't it that same middle-class self that had made nothing but wrong judgements lately? She had been wrong about Ria, wrong about Charles—and very wrong about Edward. He was good, and kind, and if he had seemed anything else, it had only been because he'd mis-judged her.

And she was in no position to fault him for that, was she?

'Olivia?'

She looked up. Edward was watching her, a curious smile on his mouth, and a look in his eyes that she'd never seen before. Why—why, he was afraid she'd turn him down, she thought in amazement, and her heart swelled with joy.

'Are you *sure* I won't have to get along on your cooking?' she asked with a mock scowl.

His eyes cleared, and he grinned. 'Cross my heart.'

Olivia sighed. 'You're impossible,' she said gently.

'You'll stay, then?'

She smiled. 'Was there ever any doubt you'd get your own way?'

Edward's mouth twisted so that, for just an instant, his smile seemed flat and false.

'Never,' he said, and then he gathered her to him and kissed her until the sun stood still.

CHAPTER ELEVEN

BY LATE afternoon, Olivia's clothing hung alongside Edward's in the spacious wardrobe in the master suite of his beach house. Seeing her things there gave her a funny feeling, something between joy and pain.

She wanted to be with him. How could she not? But moving into his home this way... She had never imagined herself doing anything like it.

There wasn't anything immoral in it. Men and women lived together outside of marriage all the time in today's world.

But Edward hadn't asked her to live with him, he'd asked her to stay with him. There was a difference. What would happen when they went back to New York and stepped into their real lives again?

Olivia sat down on the edge of the bed. What if he asked her to move into his apartment with him? Would she—could she—do it? If only she knew what he really felt for her. He had made wonderful, joyous love to her, but he'd never once said the words she longed to hear.

'...for dinner?'

She turned. Edward had popped his head out of the bathroom doorway; she could see a dollop of white shaving cream on his cheek.

'I'm sorry,' she said with a quick smile, 'I—I didn't get that.'

'I said, shall we go into town for dinner, or have it here?'

'Here,' she said immediately. 'On the terrace, so we can watch the sun set.' She looked at him and gave a little laugh. 'If that's all right with you, I mean.'

159

'Of course it's all right.' He came towards her, smiling, wiping his face with the ends of the towel that lay draped around his neck. 'You like my house, then?'

'Oh, I love...' Olivia's brows rose. 'Your house? Do you own it?'

He nodded. 'Lock, stock, and all the white sand you can track inside. I don't use it as often as I'd like, only a couple of weeks or so each winter, but... Sweetheart? What's the matter?'

'I'm having trouble absorbing all this, that's all. That this place belongs to you, along with the Manhattan apartment and the house in East Hampton.'

'There's a flat in London, too, if it matters,' Edward said with a puzzled smile. 'I go over on business several times a year, you see, and...' He shook his head. 'Maybe I missed something, Olivia. Is there a problem with my living arrangements?'

'No. No, of course not.' She stood up. 'I just—I just was thinking how very different we are, you and I.'

As different as night and day, a cold little voice deep within her hissed, but Edward's hand, sliding beneath her T-shirt, chased the voice away.

'We are that,' he said in a husky whisper. She caught her breath as his fingers skimmed lightly over her bare skin. 'Oh, yes, we definitely are different, darling. And a damned good thing it is, too.' He peered past her to the open closet, and smiled. 'I see you've commandeered all the extra hangers, hmm?'

She stiffened in his arms. 'This was your idea, Edward, remember?'

'Hey.' He tilted her face up to his. 'Something is wrong here, isn't it?'

'I'm just being stupid,' she said after a moment. 'I feel—I feel a little strange, I guess. Being here with you, I mean.'

He smiled. 'Is being with me so terrible?'

Her heart turned over. She could see herself being with him forever, that was the trouble. But Edward wasn't asking for forever, not yet. But he might, oh, yes, he might...

Men like him never ask that of girls like you, the cold voice within her whispered.

His arms went around her. 'Such a long face,' he said softly.

Olivia shook her head. 'I'm sorry, Edward. I just——'

'If you think I'd let you get away now, after all the trouble I went through to get you in my clutches...'

She couldn't help smiling as he gave a mock growl and bit her neck gently.

'You're trapped,' he said. 'I've got you, and I'm not about to set you free.'

His teasing words suddenly made her feel foolish. Why was she spoiling the happiness they'd found together with such dark thoughts? She sighed and lay her head against his shoulder.

'I get it,' she said. 'You've enticed me into your lair, and——'

'And now I'm going to keep you. Yes.'

She pressed her lips to his skin. 'How?' she whispered.

There was the briefest pause, and then Edward laughed. 'Any way I can, darling.'

There was a roughness in his voice, and she looked up quickly, half afraid he'd turn back into that dark, cold stranger who had come storming into her life a few short weeks before.

'Edward? What is it?'

He looked down at her, and for just a heartbeat his eyes seemed flat and dark, but then he smiled and brushed the hair back from her temples.

'It's just occurred to me, I've no idea if there's anything in the house for dinner.'

Olivia laughed. 'The man's always thinking of his stomach.'

'I'd better, if you're going to sap my strength day and night.' He grinned. 'Did I mention that housekeeper says that since I didn't give her notice of my arrival she won't be able to start until next week?'

She leaned back in his arms. 'Aha,' she said lightly, 'now I understand. You wanted me here so I could save you from your own awful cooking.'

'For all I know, the only thing you can cook is coffee.'

'I'll have you know I'm a world-class chef.' Olivia smiled. 'As long as there's a can opener and a freezer handy, that is. Now, come on down to the kitchen and——'

Edward shook his head. 'I'll be along in a couple of minutes. I want to shave first.'

'You just did.' She sighed dramatically. 'You'll do anything to avoid kitchen duty, won't you?'

'You caught me, darling.' He gave her a light swat on the backside. 'Let me shower and change to a pair of jeans, and I'll join you. OK?'

Her chin lifted. 'You just want me out of this room,' she said.

He went still. 'What?'

She laughed softly as she kissed his mouth. 'You're afraid I'll—how did you put it?—I'll "sap your strength" again.'

The breath puffed from his lungs. 'Exactly, darling. Now, do us both a favour and go on down to the kitchen and toss half a steer on the fire.'

Olivia smiled. 'Don't be long,' she whispered, 'all right?'

'Five minutes,' he promised, 'and not a second more.'

She hummed as she made supper. The kitchen was modern and well-equipped; she found steaks in the freezer, defrosted them in the microwave, then put them on the electric grill while she made a green salad. Half an hour later, dinner was ready—but Edward still hadn't appeared. She went to the bottom of the steps and called his name. When he didn't answer, she trotted up the stairs to the master bedroom.

'Edward?' she said, as she pushed open the half-closed door.

He was sitting on the edge of the bed, his back to her, the telephone cradled against his ear.

'Edward?' she repeated.

He looked over his shoulder, and when she saw the cold, angry look on his face she took a quick step back.

'Just do it,' he said into the phone, 'and do it quickly.'

He slammed the receiver into the cradle and took a breath. When he turned to her again, his face was composed.

'I didn't mean to intrude,' Olivia said, her eyes on his. 'But——'

'Business,' he said. He smiled tightly as he came towards her. 'It follows me everywhere.'

She nodded. 'You looked so—so angry...'

His smile tilted, then righted itself. 'Did I? Well, I guess I was. The wonderful smell of that steak was luring me downstairs, when all of a sudden the damned phone called me back.' He kissed the top of her head. 'What red-blooded man wouldn't be angry?'

Olivia tilted her head up. 'But, Edward...'

'Hush,' he whispered, and he caught her to him and kissed her fiercely, over and over, so that by the time they got to their dinner, the steak was burned to a crisp— but it didn't matter any more than the fact that the telephone couldn't have called Edward back because it had never rung.

All that mattered was the happiness filling Olivia's love-starved heart.

The time passed slowly, long tropical days of sun and sea, longer nights of moonlight and love. Nothing intruded upon their solitude, not even the soft-spoken housekeeper who arrived early in the morning and left before midday. Everything they did was ordinary, yet doing it together made it all seem wonderful and exotic, whether it was watching the fishing boats come in at

Potters Cay or seeing dolphins leap from the lagoon at Paradise Beach.

Sometimes, at night, Olivia would awaken in Edward's arms and listen to the soft whisper of the sea and the even softer sigh of his breath, and she'd try not to question if anything so wonderful could possibly last.

But the answer came anyway, on a day that seemed, at first, to be the same as any other. Edward had chartered a boat, a two-masted schooner on which they'd already visited Cat Island and beautiful San Salvador. On this day, they were making for the Exumas, a string of tiny islands and cays that Edward had promised were incredibly beautiful.

Halfway there, one of the crewmen had come on deck to tell him that he had a phone call on the radio-telephone.

Olivia saw him stiffen. 'Business,' he said, in a taut voice that took her back to the phone call she'd interrupted that very first night. She nodded and touched her hand to his cheek.

'It's all right,' she said. 'I understand.'

She waited on deck, her hair flying in the warm breeze while the boat heeled sharply under the wind, its sail bellying whitely against the cloudless blue sky. How she'd come to love these islands, she thought with a little smile. At first, she'd seen them only as glitzy tourist traps. Now, she saw them as they really were, bright jewels dropped in an azure sea, where you could, in the morning, window-shop for all the treasures of the world—and what a hard time she'd had, convincing Edward she would not permit him to buy her every lovely dress and accessory he admired—and in the afternoon dive on pink coral reefs from a beach so deserted it was easy to imagine that no one had ever seen it but you.

It was being with Edward that made the difference. How she loved him! There had to be a better word for what she felt, one that described how her heart soared each time he walked into a room or how just the sound of his voice could bring a smile to her lips. There had to be some far more complex way to describe the way her breathing quickened when their eyes met and he gave her that slow, sexy smile that meant he wanted her...

A sound caught her ear. She looked around and saw Edward stepping from the deck house.

'Hi,' she started to say—but he wasn't looking at her. Instead, he turned and walked to the lee rail, stuffed his hands in the pockets of his cut-off denims, and stood staring out to sea.

Olivia's smile faded. She couldn't see his face, but she didn't need to. There was tension in every line of his body.

A chill seemed to settle deep within her despite the hot sun as she walked slowly to where he stood.

'Edward?' She waited, then stepped beside him. 'Edward, is everything all right?'

He turned slowly and looked at her, and she caught her breath at what she saw in his eyes.

Rage. God, such rage...

But then he blinked, and smiled, and it was gone.

'Hello, darling,' he said. 'Sorry I took so long.'

'Bad news?'

'What?'

Olivia put her hand on his arm. 'I said, was the call bad news?'

'Oh. Oh, no, not—not bad news. Just...' He blew out his breath. 'Business,' he said briskly, 'you know how that can be.'

That was what he'd said last time.

'Have I mentioned that that bathing suit of yours is driving me crazy?' He slid his arms around her waist. 'There ought to be a law against beautiful women wearing things like that.'

She knew he was deliberately changing the subject. For some reason, that upset her; it was as if he were walling himself off from any questions she might ask—but then, what questions could she ask about his business? What she knew about arbitrage could be stuffed into a thimble, with room left to fit it on her finger.

'That *is* what you call that scrap of black nylon, isn't it? A bathing suit?'

Olivia looked up and managed a smile. 'Yes. Yes, it is.'

Edward smiled, too, but she thought there was a falsity to the smile. 'Well?' he said. 'What are we going to do about it?'

'I—I don't know,' she said, and he bent his head to hers, whispered into her ear while he pointed to an island ahead, an island he assured her was deserted.

And, after a while, she forgot everything but the spiralling need within her.

That evening, they stood on the terrace fronting Edward's house, sipping piña coladas.

'I've never felt so lazy,' Olivia sighed. 'It's a good thing your housekeeper left cold salad and——'

'No.'

She looked at Edward. He was standing at the terrace railing, his back to her.

'Well, then, I can grill some——'

'We're going out this evening,' he said.

'Out? But——'

'We haven't been out at night—really out—since I brought you to stay with me.'

To stay with me. Not to live with me, but to stay with me.

Olivia took a breath. 'We don't have to,' she said, 'really.'

He smiled. 'And before you tell me you've nothing suitable to wear...' He took her hand and drew her through the cool, shadowy rooms to the bedroom. 'There,' he said, pushing her gently ahead of him. 'What do you think of that?'

'That' was a gown of rose-coloured silk with tiny straps, a tucked bodice, and a softly pleated skirt. It lay spread out on their bed, and beside it were silk shoes and a bag to match. It was an outfit they had seen before, two mornings ago in the window of a chic boutique on Paradise Island.

'Someone made that dress with you in mind,' Edward had said, looping his arm around her shoulders, and Olivia had sighed.

'Someone made it with King Midas in mind,' she'd said. 'Who'd ever spend so much money on a dress?'

'I would,' had been the prompt reply, and only when she'd flatly refused to take so much as a step into the shop had Edward relented and let her tug him away from the window.

But, apparently, that hadn't been the end of it. He had bought the dress, and the matching accessories, and now they lay waiting for her.

But she felt no pleasure at the sight of the gift. She thought, instead, of how the cost of it would show up on his charge account bill the way Charles Wright's gifts to Ria had.

Lord, what was the matter with her today?

'You don't like the dress?'

'Of course I do. But you shouldn't have bought it, Edward, you...'

Her prim speech of refusal caught in her throat. How could she refuse him anything, when he was looking at her like this? She had never seen him—never *imagined* him—wearing such a vulnerable expression, as if—as if...

'Don't turn it down, darling.' He lay his hands on her shoulders and looked into her eyes. 'Tonight is special. I've reserved a table at an inn on the beach, and a suite of rooms...'

'But we have a table on the beach,' she said, smiling back at him. 'And a suite of rooms. What place could be lovelier than this?'

'Get that dress on,' he said gently. 'The plane will be here soon, and——'

'What?' She stared at him. 'You mean, we're going to dinner by plane? Edward, are you crazy?'

'I told you,' he said, 'tonight is special.'

Their eyes met. 'All right,' she said softly, 'if it's what you want...'

'It is,' he said, and how could she not agree?

The gown made her look like a princess in a fairy-tale.

'Beautiful,' Edward whispered when he saw her.

It was what she was thinking, too, looking at him, dark and dazzlingly handsome in a white dinner-jacket and dark trousers.

'Turn around,' he said softly, and when she did, he lifted up her hair and she felt the brush of his fingers against her skin. 'Now look into the mirror, darling.'

'Oh, Edward...' She fell silent. There were no words to describe the emeralds blazing at her throat. Their eyes met in the glass. 'Edward,' she whispered, 'I—I can't.'

He caught her by the shoulders and spun her to him. 'You can,' he said, almost fiercely, and he kissed her until she was breathless and clinging to him for support. Then he scooped her up into his arms, and while she laughed and begged him to put her down, he trotted out of the house and to the beach, where a little seaplane waited at the dock.

The plane took them to Eleuthera, where a white-pillared inn stood beside the sea. Edward had said everything would be perfect, but surely there had to be a better word to describe this place of candlelight, flowers, and soft violins, all of it—the musicians, the *sommelier*, the head waiter and waiters and stewards—just for them.

'Where are the other patrons?' Olivia whispered across the table, and Edward caught her hand and lifted it to his lips.

'Eating at home, I suppose,' he said, his eyes twinkling.

'But...' Her eyes widened. 'Edward? Did you—did you reserve this place just for us?'

He smiled and rose to his feet. 'Come dance with me, darling,' he said softly, and with a little smile of disbelief, she went into his arms.

There was wine waiting at the table when they returned to it, a bubbly champagne that looked like gold and tasted like magic, but why would Olivia want wine when she was already intoxicated by the feel of Edward in her arms?

A special night, he'd said, and suddenly all her doubts faded. Her heart swelled with a joy so intense it stole her breath away.

Edward had fallen in love with her, that was what this was all about. He'd fallen in love with her, and tonight—tonight, he would tell her so. That was why she'd sensed a tension in him all through the day.

Olivia's throat constricted. Edward, my love, she thought, oh, Edward, I love you so! How can I tell you, how can I show you how very much I adore you...?

'Good evening, *madame*.' She looked up. The head waiter was standing beside their table, smiling politely. 'How are you this evening?'

Happy, she thought giddily, that's how I am. Happy, happy...

'Darling?' Edward leaned towards her. 'Are you all right?'

'Oh, yes,' she said softly, 'yes, thank you. I'm fine.'

The head waiter cleared his throat. 'We have several specialities for your consideration tonight, *madame*. Our chef has prepared a crawfish and grouper chowder...'

Olivia nodded. 'All right.'

'...or perhaps *madame* would prefer melon and ham?'

What she'd prefer, she thought impatiently, was to be alone with Edward, to find some way to let him know how much he meant to her.

'And we have excellent turtle soup. The stock is freshly made, and...'

The stock. Olivia went absolutely still. The stock, she thought, the Gemini shares...

She made herself sit through the rest of the litany, nodding her head in what she hoped were the right places, agreeing to whatever the man suggested, then waiting with growing impatience until Edward had ordered his meal, too. Then she touched the tip of her tongue to her lips and leaned forward.

'Edward?' Olivia hesitated. 'We—we said we'd never mention Ria again...'

His response was swift. 'I don't want to discuss Ria, Olivia. Not now.'

'No. No, I don't either. Well, I do, in a way, but...' She smiled a little. 'I know that stock—the Gemini stock—meant a lot to you.'

A muscle knotted in his jaw. 'Olivia——'

'And—and I think you ought to have it, Edward. I mean, I think you have the right to speak to Ria and convince her——'

'Dammit.' His voice was sharp. 'Why are you intent on discussing this now?'

'Because...' She drew a breath. 'Because I—I want to help you,' she whispered. 'I *can* help you, Edward. I—I know where Ria is.' She waited for him to say something, but he just sat there, his face closed, his eyes expressionless. 'I have a postcard,' she said in a rush, 'an old one. And it has a picture on it, of a hotel and—the point is, I know in my bones that Ria's there. Here, I mean, in the islands. I couldn't find the place, but you could, Edward, you have the resources and...' She sat back in her chair. 'I should have told you days ago, I know. But when we get back to the house, I'll——'

'Crooked Island.'

His voice was flat. Olivia looked at him.

'What?' she said with a little laugh.

'Crooked Island. It's where Ria is. Fitting, isn't it? She's been there ever since she left New York.'

Olivia stared at him. 'You mean, you found her? But how? When? I don't...'

'Today. That was the call I got, on the schooner.' He lifted his wine glass and tossed down half its contents. 'My men just located her.'

'But how could they have?'

The muscle knotted in his jaw again, and he took a breath. 'I have the postcard, Olivia.'

'You don't. It's in the pocket of——'

'I took it from your suitcase the day I moved you into my house.'

Her eyes widened. 'You what?'

'I took it.' His voice was cold, his face grim. 'I knew you'd come to these islands for a damned good reason. There had to be something you knew—or had—that I didn't.'

She stared at him. 'You mean, you—you went through my things?'

'Yes.'

'Yes?' She stared at him. 'Yes? Is that all you can say? You stole it from me, Edward, you——'

'You said you weren't going to help me.'

God. Oh, God, it was all coming apart. End of discussion, he'd said when she'd tried to tell him about Ria, and it was true, there'd been no need to talk, not when he'd found a better way. Edward hadn't wanted her, he'd wanted access to whatever information she had. That was the reason he'd moved her in with him, the reason he'd said whatever he thought she wanted to hear...

'I was going to tell you tonight.'

She fought to keep from letting him see her pain.

'Were you?' she said. Her voice was without inflexion.

'Yes.' He drew a deep breath, then puffed it out. 'You see, I have to fly to New York in the morning.'

Her fingers clutched at the edge of the damask tablecloth. She understood now. Tonight was pay-off time, or kiss-off time, or whatever you called a moment like this. That was the reason for the gown, for the emeralds, for the celebratory dinner.

'I see,' she said stiffly.

'No, Olivia, dammit, you do not see!'

'Oh, but I do.' She forced herself to look at him. 'And what plans have you made for me? You have made plans for me, Edward, haven't you?'

His brows drew together. 'I doubted you'd want to go along,' he said slowly. 'You're welcome to stay in the beach house until...'

Her stomach rose in her throat and she shoved her chair back from the table and lurched to her feet.

'Olivia?' His chair scraped as he pushed it back. 'Olivia! Where in hell do you think you're going?'

'Stay away from me, Edward,' she said in a shaky whisper. Her fingers went to her throat and she snatched the emeralds loose and tossed them on to the table. 'Just stay away!'

'Olivia, dammit——'

'Sir? Is there a problem?'

The head waiter stepped between them just as Edward got to his feet. It was the edge she needed and she took it, turning and running swiftly through the restaurant while the waiters gaped and the music stopped in mid-phrase.

Where do you think you're going? Edward had demanded. Well, she knew where she was going. She was going as far from this place, and this man, as she could manage. She had tried doing that before, but he had caught up with her and her life had never been the same since.

This time would be different. This time, as she jumped into a waiting taxi, she wasn't fool enough to give the driver any directions other than the one that would set her free.

'To the airport,' she said breathlessly, and as the cab shot from the kerb she turned and saw Edward burst out through the door and stand helplessly in the roadway as she sped off into the night.

CHAPTER TWELVE

OLIVIA began to think straight five minutes into the journey. How could she get on a plane, dressed like this? It was still wintertime back in New York; for all she knew there was snow on the streets.

Besides, she had to get the marks of Edward's possession off her body. The gown, the shoes... She leaned forward and cleared her throat.

'I need to change what I'm wearing,' she said. 'Is there anyplace open at this hour where I can buy some clothing?'

The cabbie looked into his rear-view mirror, saw her pale, stricken face, and asked no questions. Moments later, they pulled up at an open-air market, still thronged with laughing tourists, and Olivia took the Cinderella story full circle.

She stepped into the market a princess and came out a commoner, but then that was what she'd always been.

The housekeeper's niece, she thought, and bile rose in her throat. Ria had known it all along, and so had Edward. The only one who'd been foolish enough to think otherwise had been Olivia herself, but that was all over now.

The airport was busy, despite the hour. People were coming and going, all of them laughing and happy. She felt like a pariah in their midst but nobody paid any attention to her at all, not even the ever-smiling reservations clerk who said yes, there was an empty seat on the next flight to New York and then compounded that miracle by accepting Olivia's Visa card for payment. Surely she had long since exceeded her credit limit.

Not that it mattered. Soon she'd be knee-deep in bankruptcy if Olivia's Dream didn't survive the scandal.

And at this moment, she didn't much give a damn whether it did or...

The hair rose on the nape of her neck. She turned—and there he was—Edward, striding through the terminal towards the gate at which she waited, tall and imposing and darkly handsome, marching along as if he owned the world and with a look of such dark rage on his face that it made her blood run cold.

Heads swivelled in his wake; whispers flew after him. But he was oblivious to all of it, the raised eyebrows, the admiring glances of the women and the assessing ones of the men. He was intent on only one thing, and that was finding Olivia.

She shrank back into the shadows of a closed ticket counter, then shrank back again until her shoulders were pressed against the wall. She knew why he wanted to find her—it didn't take any great effort to figure it out. Women didn't walk out on Edward Archer, especially women like her. He hadn't been quite ready to dismiss her yet, not when there was still one long night left before his departure, all those hours before dawn when she could lie in his arms and let him dominate her with his passion.

'Oh, God!'

The whispered imprecation spilled from her lips. Olivia put the back of her hand to her mouth. She could not, would not, let him force her into a confrontation. She had run from him, yes, but the act had made him as much a loser in this hideous game they'd played as she. She had no intention of giving up the little advantage that had accrued to her and no wish to see him again, to look into those eyes that had seen her naked and vulnerable and see only coldness and smug satisfaction.

It wasn't easy, evading him. But she had everything on her side. She had seen Edward before he saw her, and she was dressed not in the expensive trappings he'd layered upon her but in baggy white trousers, canvas flats, a voluminous cotton shirt with an equally vol-

uminous jacket over it. She had a hat, too, a floppy
canvas sun-hat with a deep brim, bought more to shield
her red-rimmed eyes from the curiosity of strangers than
for any other reason. Now, with trembling fingers, she
pulled it off, tucked her hair on top of her head, then
dragged the hat on again.

The disguise wasn't much, but it was all she could
manage.

At last, he came to a stop, hands on hips, legs slightly
apart, head elevated. He looked cold and dangerous;
several people made a detour around him like fish
swimming carefully around a shark. Olivia stood back
and waited in the shadows.

When her flight was called, she stepped forward
quickly, blending into a laughing group of men and
women who seemed determined to go on partying until
faced with the cool light of a Manhattan dawn.

'Hey, sweetie!' The man closest to her grinned and
clamped a meaty arm around her shoulders. He blew a
heavy miasma of rum into her pale face. 'Where'd you
come from, hmm?'

Olivia forced a smile to her face. 'Hi,' she said, and
she wrapped her arm around his waist. She leaned into
him, letting his beefy body shield hers as they made their
way towards the ramp. She sensed when they passed
Edward: the breath seemed to whoosh from her lungs
and she swayed unsteadily in the stranger's grasp.

'Easy does it.' The man giggled. 'I know just how you
feel, babe. Hang on tight and let ol' Billy get you safely
on board.'

He did. But the tension didn't leave her, not even when
the cabin doors were secured nor when the plane began
taxiing towards the runway. And even when the night
sky swallowed them up and the seatbelt signs blinked
off, Olivia's fingers still lay twisted together in her lap.

'Hey, babe,' a voice said, and she looked up and saw
the man who'd boarded with her making his way down
the aisle. 'How's it goin'?'

'Fine,' she said, and she even managed a quick smile as he edged past.

But she was not fine, she was broken inside, she was holding herself together as if she were a crystal that would fracture into a million pieces if she let go.

Edward had done this to her.

How had she ever let herself believe she loved him?

She took a steadying breath. All right, she thought, that's enough. She was all grown up now. She wasn't going to lock herself in her room and cry her heart out because a man like Edward Archer had used her. She was stronger than that.

To hell with him. She didn't need him. She had herself. Herself, and Olivia's Dream.

It wasn't gone. Not yet. All this time she'd stumbled around, letting first a rag like the *Chatterbox* and then Edward Archer throw her into a panic when what she should have been doing was fighting to hang on to what was rightly hers. She had resources. Charles had forgiven her the money he'd lent her. And, until the courts or the banks took it from her, she had the town house. She had other things, too, less tangible but every bit as real. Skill. Talent. Training. And the dogged determination that had led her from the servants' quarters in the Bascomb house to Olivia's Dream.

You'll lose it, Edward had said; it was one of the threats that had forced her into his trap. Well, maybe she would, but not without a fight. Edward couldn't know how important Olivia's Dream was to her, that it represented not only financial security but respectability.

'Ladies and gentlemen, the captain has asked me to remind you to please raise your seat-backs and fasten your belts. Thanks to a strong tail wind, we'll be landing in New York fifteen minutes ahead of schedule.'

And not a moment too soon, Olivia thought with determination. She had a life to put together, and precious little time in which to do it.

*   *   *

The phone rang at six, just as she awakened. Olivia was certain she knew who it was and she shrank back against the pillows and let it ring and ring until finally it fell silent. But it rang again ten minutes later, then every five minutes until she finally switched on the answering machine she'd turned off after the first crank calls weeks before.

When the phone rang again, she stood beside it, trembling as she listened to Edward's cold, furious demands that she take his call.

'Damn you, Olivia, you can't get away with this!'

But she could. All she had to do was remember how much she hated him. And she did. God, she did.

When his call ended, she grabbed the phone and dialled Dulcie.

'Olivia! Where've you been? I've called and called, but—— '

'How would you like to come back to work, Dulcie?'

'Oh, I'd love it! That's one of the reasons I've been phoning, to see what you want to do. Have you been looking at the *Chatterbox*? There hasn't been a word in it about—well, about the whole mess, not for days. So I thought maybe——'

'You thought right. There's only one problem.' Olivia rubbed her forehead. 'I don't have any money to pay your salary. You'd have to be willing to work on commission until things pick up. When they do—if they do—I'll pay you the wages I owe you plus a bonus, and——'

'OK.'

Olivia's brows lifted. 'Are you sure?'

'Look, we'll give it a month. I can manage that. And then, if things aren't any better...' Dulcie cleared her throat. 'When do you want me to come in?'

Olivia smiled for the first time in almost twenty-four hours. 'How does five minutes ago sound?'

Dulcie showed up an hour later. She gave Olivia a hug, then stepped back and stared at her.

'My gosh, look at you! You're so tan—have you been away?'

'Yes. The Bahamas.'

'The Bahamas!' The other girl rolled her eyes. 'Why not? If there's no way to save the ship, you might as well party while it goes down.'

'That's not why I . . .' She looked at Dulcie, who knew nothing of Ria or her involvement in what had happened, and she gave a little laugh. 'It's a long story,' she said. 'Remind me to tell it to you some time.'

Dulcie smiled. 'Just tell me about the hot sun, tropical moonlight, and gorgeous guys. I bet you had a terrific time.'

The women's eyes met and suddenly, to her horror, Olivia felt her own fill with tears. She swung away quickly.

'Olivia?' The other girl touched her shoulder. 'What is it? Did I say the wrong thing?'

Olivia shook her head. 'No, don't be silly. I just—I got in late, that's all. I—I didn't get much sleep.'

'Are you sure?'

Olivia wiped the back of her hand across her eyes, then turned and gave Dulcie a bright smile.

'Positive. Now, let's get down to business.'

They spent the afternoon going through their records. The next day, Olivia began phoning potential customers who'd vanished after the Charles Wright mess hit the *Chatterbox*.

The first calls were difficult. 'Hello,' she said brightly, as if there'd never been a question but that the project would go to her design studio, 'this is Olivia's Dream calling. We wondered if you'd made a decision about your living-room.'

Or dining-room or summer house. Whatever. And then she waited, fingers crossed, for an answer.

No one hung up on her. No one leaped at the chance to come in and sign a contract, either. But several people said, well, they hadn't actually reached a decision, not just yet. And three made appointments to come in during the week and talk.

Her success gave her courage. She took a breath, drew the phone to her, and started dialling again. These calls were tougher: they went to customers who'd cancelled orders after the scandal had broken.

People did hang up this time. But others said they had not made new arrangements, and made appointments then and there. Still others came strolling into the shop days later.

By the end of the week, things were looking up. Olivia's Dream had clients again, not enough to make a profit but enough to give hope that it might just survive. Olivia was putting in twelve-hour days, designing, sketching, sweet-talking creditors into extensions and indulging in what Dulcie labelled creative bookkeeping.

She was also, Dulcie said late in the second week, working herself to a frazzle.

'You can't keep this up forever,' she insisted just before she trotted down the stairs to the show room.

Olivia put down her pencil and rubbed her temples wearily. It was true, she was exhausted. But it wasn't the days that were draining her. It was the nights, the long, empty hours of darkness. That was when the world seemed to tilt, when all her courage failed her and she couldn't stop thinking about Edward or stop dreaming of him, long, sensual dreams in which he took her in his arms and made love to her.

Even in the dreams, she wanted to stop him. I hate you, Edward, she wanted to say, don't touch me.

But she never did. Instead, she gave herself up to him in ecstasy and when she awoke to reality her heart would ache even more because the dreams only proved how really weak she was when it came to fighting against desire.

At least he had given up phoning. After all, what was the point in raging at an answering machine? And his rage had run its course now—if it hadn't, he'd have tried to force his way in to see her. Well, it was a good thing he hadn't. She'd have—she'd have...

'Olivia?' Olivia looked up. Dulcie was standing in the doorway, looking stricken. 'The postman just brought this.'

It was an envelope from Charles Wright's attorney and marked 'registered mail'. Olivia ripped it open and drew out a sheet of paper. She scanned it quietly, then looked at Dulcie.

'It says I'm overdue paying off my loan.'

'Are you?'

Olivia shook her head. There was no loan, not any more. Charles Wright's will had taken care of that. Surely, his lawyer knew that.

'It's a mistake,' she said. 'I'll take care of it.'

She telephoned the lawyer. He was pleasant and almost apologetic. He'd had no choice but to send the letter, he explained, all things considered.

'There was a codicil, Miss Harris, you're correct. But it's being contested.'

'By whom?' she asked.

But it wasn't necessary. She knew the answer before the attorney offered it.

'By Wright's stepson, Edward Archer.'

Olivia closed her eyes. 'Because of the stock bequest to Ria Bascomb,' she said softly.

'You know about that?' The man sighed. 'Actually, that's all taken care of. Archer located Miss Bascomb. He made arrangements with her that satisfied them both.'

'Well, then, I don't understand...?'

The lawyer cleared his throat. 'He's contesting the will because of the bequest his stepfather made to you, my dear. Even if his challenge is denied, I'm afraid it may be some time before you gain any relief from the obligation.'

Olivia managed some polite response, but her heart was pounding. How dared Edward do this to her? He'd

got what he'd wanted, he had control of the stock—
what more did he want? Was he demanding the collapse
of Olivia's Dream as payment for her having walked out
on him in the Bahamas?

Well, he wasn't going to get it, not if she had anything
to say about it, and she was going to tell him that this
very minute. She glanced at her watch. He was probably
at his office. Would his business address be listed in the
phone directory under his own name?

It was. Olivia scribbled it down, snatched up her bag,
and clattered down the stairs.

His offices were on the seventy-fifth floor of a towering
glass and steel skyscraper in the lower reaches of
Manhattan. It was the kind of setting that whispered
money, power, and prestige. It was designed to be, and
was, in fact, intimidating. But Olivia was beyond in-
timidation. She was angry, and anger propelled her out
of the lift and to a burled walnut reception desk. It got
her beyond that desk and down a long hallway—but
then, as she stood outside a door marked with Edward's
name, her courage gave way.

What did she think she was going to accomplish?
Edward could do as he liked; she couldn't stop him. He
had everything on his side, while she—she . . .

The door swung open and she found herself looking
up into his familiar, handsome face, and in that instant
she knew the truth.

It wasn't fear of losing Charles's bequest that had sent
her here. It was the simple fact that she loved Edward,
despite what he was and what he'd done to her. She had
loved him in the Bahamas, she loved him now, she would
always love him. And what did that make her, if not the
greatest idiot the world had ever known?

She took a quick step back, and Edward reached out
and caught hold of her. His touch was coolly impersonal, but there was no withdrawing from it. There was
steel in his fingers and in the way he was looking at her.

'Come inside, Olivia,' he said coldly. 'It's too late to run this time.'

Her heart was racing, but she lifted her chin, shrugged off his hand, and strode past him as if that was what she'd intended all the time.

His office was huge, almost as large as her entire flat. The furnishings were handsome, she was certain, but she couldn't pay them any attention. All she could think of was that she'd done this to herself, she'd come here of her own volition, and now she was trapped.

'Sit down,' he said.

She turned towards him. He had closed the door and now he was leaning back against it, his arms crossed over his chest, watching her with virtually no expression on his face.

'No, thank you,' she said calmly, although the pounding of her pulse was beating in her ears. 'What I have to say won't take very long.'

A cat-like smile curled across his mouth. 'I know why you've come, of course.'

'Yes.' She swallowed. 'Yes, I'm sure you do.'

'The bequest in Wright's will—you want to know why you still have to pay back the loan.'

Olivia drew herself up. 'I know the reason, Edward. You've contested it.'

He nodded. 'Yes. That's right, I have.'

'Even though you have the stock you wanted.'

'Your friend was most eager to sell it at market value, Olivia, once I assured her I had no interest in dragging her name through the mud.'

'Well, that must have simplified things. I mean, if I'd been the one to find her, I couldn't have made her such an offer, could I? I'd have wanted her to—to stand up and shout to the world that it was she who'd had an affair with your stepfather, not me.'

Edward looked at her for a long moment, and then he leaned away from the door and walked slowly towards her.

'Would you really have done that?' he asked softly. 'Ria asked me if you were angry, and I told her you were, yes, that your friendship would never be the same again, but that I doubted if you wanted revenge.'

'Did you really?' Olivia said furiously. 'Well, you shouldn't have spoken for me, Edward. I—I . . .' She fell silent, and then she sighed. 'No,' she said after a couple of seconds, 'I don't want revenge. I thought I did, at first, but . . .' She wet her lips. 'Is she all right?'

'She's fine. She panicked, apparently; she was afraid of what her family would say when they realised she'd been living with Wright. For whatever it's worth, he'd told her he'd begged my mother for a divorce and she'd refused.'

'But he hadn't,' Olivia said softly.

'No.' His voice was clipped; when he smiled, it was cold and without humour. 'But Ria Bascomb wasn't the first young woman to fall for old Charlie's line.'

Olivia nodded. 'Well, then, you have what you wanted.'

Edward's eyes narrowed. 'Have I?'

'Yes. The Gemini stock. You said Ria signed it over to you . . .'

He stepped forward quickly, before she could move back, and caught her roughly by the shoulders.

'Why did you run away from me?'

Olivia gave a nervous laugh. 'Did I spoil your evening, Edward? Would you like me to apologise?'

'I don't understand you,' he said gruffly. 'I don't think I ever will. You're the most independent woman I've ever known; you've made it in this world on your own, and yet you keep turning tail and running like a frightened rabbit.'

'Never!' Colour rose under her skin. 'That's a lie. I never run!'

'You've been so busy running you never took the time to see the truth.'

'When did I run?' she demanded. 'Just give me one example.'

His eyes locked on hers. 'You ran from my apartment that night, weeks ago.'

'I did not!'

'You wanted to go to bed with me, but the idea scared the hell out of you, so you bolted.'

'Let go of me,' she demanded. 'I didn't come here to be insulted.'

'You ran that day in East Hampton, when we were going to make love.'

'Is that what you call what we were going to do?' she said, struggling futilely against his iron grasp. 'I should think there's a far better word to describe it.'

'And you ran that night in the Bahamas——'

'God, Edward, what an enormous ego you have! What's the problem, hmm? Am I the first woman who's walked out on you?'

'Dammit, Olivia, will you stop behaving like an idiot and listen to me?'

'Listen to whom? An arrogant, insufferable bastard who'll stop at nothing when he thinks he's been thwarted?'

'I'm trying to tell you that I'm in love with you, you bloody little fool!' Edward's fingers bit into her flesh. 'God knows why; you're probably going to make my life a misery and me a wreck, you'll drive me to drink or worse. But I can't help it, I'm in love with you and I have been for weeks. Hell, for all I know, I've been in love with you from that minute you spilled whiskey on me in that restaurant.' His voice roughened. 'The same day I spotted my stepfather drooling all over you.'

'He wasn't drooling,' Olivia said breathlessly. 'I told you——'

'Yeah. You did. But I was too jealous to listen.' Edward's arms slipped around her. 'I thought you loved me, too. You said you did, that night in the Bahamas.'

'Edward——'

'Do you love me?' he demanded. 'Don't think you're going to run out before you give me an answer, Olivia. If I have to, I'll lock you inside this office for the next month and a half!'

Her heart was still racing, but now it was doing other things, too, little flips and dips and flutters. Did he mean it? Her gaze swept across his face. He was giving her a hard, dark look—but there was something in his eyes that suggested he was holding something wonderful and precious in his arms, that he wanted to kiss her and kiss her and never stop...

...which was exactly the way she felt, the way she'd been feeling all these days and weeks...

'Well?' Edward said gruffly. 'I want a simple yes or no, Olivia. Do you love me or don't you?'

She drew a deep breath. 'Why did you steal that postcard from me, Edward? I'd have given it to you. I was *going* to give it to you, that night. That's what I was trying to tell you when—when——'

'Remember what you said when I found you? "I'm not going to help you find Ria", you told me.' His eyes darkened. 'And then you asked me if I'd come to the Bahamas because I wanted to find you—or because I wanted to find Ria.' He drew a sharp breath. 'You made it sound like such a simple question, my darling, but it was as deep as the riddle of the Sphinx. And I was afraid, no matter how I answered it, I might damage the happiness we'd found in each other's arms.'

Olivia shook her head. 'Edward,' she whispered, 'I don't understand.'

He sighed. 'I'd go to the ends of the earth after you, sweetheart—but the truth was that I'd gone to the islands because I had to find Ria, too. I had no choice. That damned stock—it didn't mean much financially, but if my mother had learned that Wright left it to Ria...' He sighed again. 'It was bad enough she had to read all that crap about his "love nest". But to find out that he'd given away stock she'd given him as a token of her love...'

'You didn't want her hurt.'

Edward nodded grimly. 'I'd stalled for as much time as I could by convincing her to visit her sister in Florida after Wright's death, but I knew that, sooner or later, the will had to be formally read.' He drew a deep breath. 'All I could think of was getting that stock back before that happened.'

Olivia leaned back in his arms. 'But how can having the stock change things? I mean, if the will is read, the bequest will still be in it.'

Edward smiled tightly. 'There's not much sense in reading a codicil if it no longer has any meaning. It took a while, but I finally managed to convince Wright's attorney to go along with me on that.'

'Yes,' Olivia said, smiling a little. 'I can imagine. You can be very convincing, when you want to be.'

His hands slipped up to frame her face. 'Then let me convince you now,' he said softly. 'I love you, Olivia, I love you with all my heart. Tell me you love me, too.'

'But—but why didn't you tell me all this that morning in the Bahamas? I'd have understood.'

'Maybe.' Edward's mouth thinned. 'But I couldn't run the risk. I was too afraid of losing you.'

'And—and that last night, when you told me you'd taken the card...' She swallowed hard. 'You seemed so—so cold, Edward, so controlled.'

'Controlled?' She caught her breath as he lifted her face to him and kissed her deeply. When finally he drew back, they were both shaken. 'I'm never controlled when I'm with you, Olivia. Hell, I was desperate. I was going to propose to you that night, but just look at the things I had to tell you: that I'd gone through your luggage, that I'd found the postcard and taken it——'

'That you were leaving me behind and going to New York.'

'That was part of my deal with Ria. My people let slip that you were in the islands, looking for her, and I think she became frantic at the thought of having to face you. She would only agree to meet with me—alone—in New York.'

'And contesting the will. Why did you do that?'

'You wouldn't take my calls. I thought about confronting you—hell, I spent a couple of nights standing in the cold, outside your house.' He smiled. 'But I didn't want to take any chances. I wanted to see you on my ground, darling, with the odds all in my favour.'

Olivia's eyes filled with tears, not of sorrow but of joy. 'Oh, Edward,' she whispered, 'I've been such a fool.'

'What you are,' he said sternly, 'is an absolutely impossible woman. I asked you two simple questions an eternity ago, and I still haven't had an answer.'

Olivia rose up and pressed her mouth to his. 'Ask them again,' she whispered against his lips.

Edward looked to the ceiling. 'And she's forgetful, too. What am I going to do with her?'

'You'll think of something,' she said, smiling at him. 'Now, ask me those questions.'

His arms went around her again. 'Question one, Miss Harris. Do you love me?'

'Yes,' she sighed, 'even though you're an arrogant, insufferable man who——'

'And will you marry me?'

Her heart soared. 'When?'

Edward smiled and lifted her into his arms. 'Now,' he said, 'this very minute—or as soon as you can make arrangements to get away from Olivia's Dream.'

Olivia linked her arms around his neck. 'You foolish man,' she whispered. 'Don't you know? You're Olivia's dream.'

And he always would be.

HARLEQUIN ◈ PRESENTS®

Can you bear the heat!

Our sizzling series of the hottest stories continues....

They're

Coming next month:

Dangerous Alliance by Helen Bianchin
Harlequin Presents #1741

"Is the idea of marriage to me so unacceptable?"

If Dimitri Kostakidas had asked Leanne that question years
ago when she was an impressionable girl who fancied herself
in love with him, the answer might have been a different
one. Now she would do anything rather than share Dimitri's
bed. But there was no choice in the matter and no escape
from the future he had mapped out for her....

Available in May wherever Harlequin books are sold.

MILLION DOLLAR SWEEPSTAKES (III)

No purchase necessary. To enter the sweepstakes and receive the Free Books and Surprise Gift, follow the directions published and complete and mail your "Win A Fortune" Game Card. If not taking advantage of the book and gift offer or if the "Win A Fortune" Game Card is missing, you may enter by hand-printing your name and address on a 3" X 5" card and mailing it (limit: one entry per envelope) via First Class Mail to: Million Dollar Sweepstakes (III) "Win A Fortune" Game, P.O. Box 1867, Buffalo, NY 14269-1867, or Million Dollar Sweepstakes (III) "Win A Fortune" Game, P.O. Box 609, Fort Erie, Ontario L2A 5X3. When your entry is received, you will be assigned sweepstakes numbers. To be eligible entries must be received no later than March 31, 1996. No liability is assumed for printing errors or lost, late or misdirected entries. Odds of winning are determined by the number of eligible entries distributed and received.

Sweepstakes open to residents of the U.S. (except Puerto Rico), Canada, Europe and Taiwan who are 18 years of age or older. All applicable laws and regulations apply. Sweepstakes offer void wherever prohibited by law. Values of all prizes are in U.S. currency. This sweepstakes is presented by Torstar Corp., its subsidiaries and affiliates, in conjunction with book, merchandise and/or product offerings. For a copy of the official rules governing this sweepstakes offer, send a self-addressed, stamped envelope (WA residents need not affix return postage) to: MILLION DOLLAR SWEEPSTAKES (III) Rules, P.O. Box 4573, Blair, NE 68009, USA.

SWP-H495

HARLEQUIN®

PRESENTS: Plus

An affair...with her own husband? Laura and Dirk had been separated but, all of a sudden, he was back in her life and pursuing her. Laura couldn't forget that she had been unable to conceive Dirk's child, which meant there could be no long-term future for them—so why was she still tempted to accept his simply *outrageous* proposal!

Nell was wary of men, until she met Ben Rigby and found herself longing for something more. But she was afraid. Her child—her lost child, whom she'd never had the chance to see—shared the same birthday as Ben's adopted son...was Fate being cruel or kind?

Harlequin Presents Plus—where
women's dreams come true!

Coming next month:

An Outrageous Proposal by Miranda Lee
Harlequin Presents Plus #1737

and

Shadow Play by Sally Wentworth
Harlequin Presents Plus #1738

Harlequin Presents Plus
The best has just gotten better!

Available in May wherever Harlequin books are sold.